Cry Heaven, Cry Hell

by

Howard Gordon

CCB Publishing
British Columbia, Canada

Cry Heaven, Cry Hell

Copyright ©2014 by Howard Gordon
ISBN-13 978-1-77143-117-0
First Edition

Library and Archives Canada Cataloguing in Publication
Gordon, Howard, 1942-, author
Cry heaven, cry hell / by Howard Gordon -- First edition.
Issued in print and electronic formats.
ISBN 978-1-77143-117-0 (pbk.).--ISBN 978-1-77143-118-7 (pdf)
Additional cataloguing data available from Library and Archives Canada

Cover artwork credits: ©TpaBMa, ©asado, ©maryp, ©soleilc, ©darrenwh
courtesy of CanStockPhoto.com

Publisher: CCB Publishing
              British Columbia, Canada
              www.ccbpublishing.com

Cry Heaven,
Cry Hell

Introduction

There is only one earth. It is composed of evil and good. Perhaps it started in the Garden of Eden with the Tree of Knowledge. Perhaps there are genes for good and evil. And then maybe we learn from our elders, peers, and experience a way of conducting our affairs. To accomplish worthy acts, we pave our road to hell. To avoid this road, we may sprinkle a few redeeming behaviors in amongst the rot. Al Capone found employment for Italian immigrants while he butchered many. Josef Stalin murdered millions, but he kicked Hitler out of Russia.

In this novel, I have created three characters that combine high ideals with low life behaviors and rages that originated in their past. Craine Mikawber killed people in his native Ireland and brought a criminal career to the United States. Rodin LaMonde brings a hatred that spans the French and Indian wars for something done to his family and sought revenge by trying to weaken the French empire. Donny Clippingbird was saved from a bleak future on the reservation by being adopted by a Boston elite family. He used his influence to destroy white power. Their consciences become intrigued with building a museum dedicated to war dead of both sides.

However, one cannot teach an old dog new tricks and they find themselves using methods with which they grew up to achieve their ends. It is our judgment whether they do more harm than good and if their fates need to be determined by existing legal framework or by a framework that weighs good against evil. Is the law of our forefathers applicable or is our democratic life being threatened by new concepts by the word "terrorist"?

As has been said previously, there is only one earth. We cannot make it into 200 models, but we can structure it so that is has some flexibility for the people who populate it. Our forefathers devised laws that they felt defined a free society ruled by law not mob. They built in protective structures, but these structures became repressive and are growing in dictatorial aspects. At this point in our history maybe we should ask ourselves whether or not we want to follow in these directions. Hopefully, these three caricatures will provide a base for such decision making.

Section I

Craine Mikawber

Chapter 1

It was November of 1914. The world was at war. Ireland was shaking with rage at its exploitation by the English lords. The mess had started centuries ago, when the screaming Tudor woman had colonized them and used them to defeat Spain. Through the following centuries, famines were excuses for the bloody royals to seize their lands and rob them blind by taking the income and produce. There had also been fighting between Protestants and Catholics, maybe because England was a Protestant nation and the Prots wanted to be linked to England for protection. At any rate, a Protestant community flourished in Belfast, and Greens and Oranges fought some pretty fierce battles. The Mikawber family was pretty outspoken and were said to show a little Orange when they lost their tempers or yelled. Tyndall Mikawber and his five sons, McTavish, Oleander, Brython, Michael, and Craine stood for the Auld Orange and resisted the recently formed gangs of Sinn Fein that looked for Prot sacrifices to their pagan altar.

Craine was on his way to Greg Moriarity's grocery with a shopping list. It was a family rule since Mum had died two years ago, that the first one home had to do the shopping. Across the street, Craine saw several boys that had accompanied their fathers to Sinn Fein meetings. They knew what he was about and circled around the door to the grocery. He crossed the street, he heard, "Good morrow, me Prot laddie. Would ye like to accompany me to the true Church of a Sunday or do ye plan to continue yer present devilment?" "Up yer arse, Lobsterback," was Craine's hot reply. The boys advanced and one of them had a razor. Craine was not new at this game, and he pulled out his knife and said, "O.K., let's have at it then."

As the boys advanced on each other, Craine gulped because he well knew that one or both of them could end up stuck for eternity and stone cold dead. The decision was made, as neither was backing down. How one came to God seemed to be the major issue. A human life had no meaning in the decision about how a person or a nation came to the Lord. Each one felt he was fighting for the right way to approach God and would be blessed for fighting for the right way.

The Sinn Fein youth slashed out, and Craine ducked and fell to his knees. He slashed at his opponent's leg. "Take that one back to your priest, Boyo," he sniggered. He was yanked backward by a pair of hands and held lying on his back. The knife bearer was sitting on him and slashed his face in the rage that followed the leg wound. Another boy tried it on Craine's legs but Tyndall's son knew more about fighting and kicked him in the face. He bridged up by putting his crown down on the ground and struggling to raise his chest, toppling his assailant off of him. Quickly he got to his feet and reached for his knife, as his opponent did the same.

Both of them prepared to stab the other, and the other young men tried to get the knife away from Craine, as he slashed out. Some of them caught a slash in the process. Suddenly Craine felt a pair of strong arms around him forcing his knife hand down; as did the other fellow. He heard a familiar voice holler out, "Hold on me fighting colt," and recognized the voice of his brother, Brython. Oleander held his opponent. The other boys scattered. McTavish, Michael, and Tyndall had happened along after finishing helping a neighbor paint his barn. Tyndall brought the two boys together asking for an explanation of the events that brought four or five boys to attack his son and to bring the issue of knives to the forefront. After he heard the explanation from both sides, he asked the boy his name. The answer he got was that he didn't feel obliged to share his name with a Protestant heretic. He answered the lad with a statement that heretic or not, he was entitled to respect because he was the boy's elder and because he had spoken respectfully to the youth even though he had a knife to his son.

The youngster answered just as saucily as before: "If ye can't come to God in the right way, me Da taught me that ye ain't worth wastin' no courtesy on, grown or otherwise." Tyndall replied, "So that's the way of it. Well, we can also be rude. McTavish come here.

You're the family artist, aren't you?" His eldest son acknowledged the question affirmatively. "Well, we need your help with a brush and orange and black paint. Oleander, you hold his arms; Michael, you hold his legs. Brython pull his trousers down. McTavish, start painting his face orange, and we'll figure out the rest."

What was figured out was that after oranging up his face, the young miscreant was flipped over on his stomach, and a picture of St. Patrick chasing the snakes out of Ireland was painted on his posterior. His clothing was put in a tree and tied around a thick branch too high for him to climb. A note was attached to him explaining about the attack and that every person, including Romish Pagans was entitled to courtesy. After all we're all Irishmen and want to be free of the English bull. Freedom would come eventually. However, violence was not the answer.

The boy's name was Delphious Ornam, and his family not only did not accept Tyndall's correction, but vowed revenge against the Protestant hog.

Chapter 2

Delphious told his father, mother and ten brothers about the nervy Prot family that had let him endure a cut on his leg. They were proud of their little Catholic fighter that gave the heretic a slash on the face, before they insulted him with their insults to their real faith to their God that acknowledge the Holy Father of all Christendom, and their beautiful rituals. The family all agreed that the swine had to pay. But what revenge; what would their priest and the Father, Son, and Mother Mary demand of them. They would surely have to discuss this with Fr. Wrigley and make a sound decision about it.

That Wednesday they met with the Priest. Father felt that a house that opposed throwing the Brits out of Ireland and defied the true road to God at the same time did not deserve to stand, but he could not participate because our Lord regards violence between men as not to be the mutual love Christianity preached .He also said what he did not know could not be sent to the Lord's ears.

The Ornams had a family meeting to decide how to handle the Mikawbers. The father knew an employee of the factory where McTavish worked with his brothers, Brython and Oleander. One of his sons went to school with Michael and could detain him. The father would detain Tyndall at Avery's Pub with a discussion about settling the differences between the two families. Likewise the three brothers could be taken out of the picture by joining their employee at another pub to celebrate the end of the workday. This left Craine alone in the house. The target date was Friday night of this week. The Ornams did not want too much time to elapse before they struck back. What stuck in Jesse Ornam's craw was the picture of St. Patrick on his son's arse. They'd pay for that one.

At 5:00 p.m. Jesse met Tyndall and suggested that they talk over some ales at Avery's. Killiam engaged Michael in a friendly game of Rugby set up with two teams previously. One of the teams was short a man. He was interested in offering a gesture that the families could still be friends since no real physical harm had been done. After all, they were both still Irish, and there was more love between them than for the Brits. Tandry Obrits invited McTavish, Brython, and Oleander for a couple of cold ones and a game of darts at O'Donnell's to separate themselves from the monotonous work day. The stage was set.

In November dusk and darkness come early. Six Ornams went to the Mikawber House with a bucket of live coals and another 3 buckets of horse feces . Delphious knocked on the door with two brothers behind him. They grabbed Craine and pinned him down, picked him up and carried him to a tree, tore off his clothes, and tied him to the tree. Delphious used a pair of tongs to hold the coals that burnt Craine's face, arms and legs, and genitals. He told him they did not want him to suffer too much and rubbed the horse feces all over him to cool him. They smeared the second bucket all over the outside of the house and the third all over the inside.

Tyndall recognized that something phony was going on at Avery's because Jesse never had much to say to him, and the time was too close to the time of the painting prank. McTavish had had differences with Tandry. They were also not very friendly, especially since he gave him a black eye a year ago over starting a union at the factory. Michael was suspicious of being invited to a Rugby game by a kid with whom he felt no friendship, and whose son had painted a family member orange and put one of their saints on his rear end. However, when the game was legitimate and involved both Prots and Lobsterbacks, he joined in.

The game was short lived because one of the players fell and broke his leg on a play. The Ornams thought they kept him away long enough for their family to get their business done. They bade Michael farewell and chuckled to themselves when he was out of earshot on the way home. Likewise Tyndall and the other boys left their rendezvous early because they didn't feel comfortable with their company.

When they got home, they found Craine unconscious and smelling of horseshit, as well the inside and outside of the house. Tyndall brought his son to consciousness and asked what happened. He choked back his rage and dispatched the four boys to clean the house, while he cleaned up Craine and got the wagon ready to take him to the hospital to heal the burns. He promised a family meeting after he got back.

Once at the hospital, Dr. Bailen examined Craine and told the father that his son would have to stay in the hospital three weeks. He wanted to try a new technique called skin grafting with which they had been having successes. He diagnosed the lad with 2nd degree burns on his face and arms, and genitals.

Two days after Craine was admitted to the hospital, the Mikawbers had to get their anger out and develop a plan. McTavish was the hottest under the collar. He wanted to clean up the shotgun, steal a cannon from the armory, and blow the Ornams to smithereens. He also had a cache of dynamite that he wanted to use. Tyndall was against any killing. "We are not animals. I may be more patient than The Catholics, but I want the same freedom from the Brits that they do. Most of us Prots want the protection of England, but I've always fought my own battles. Besides if you take someone's help there's always a price to pay. I don't feel like being pushed into that war overseas. It's going to be one bloody, long thing, and we'll never be the same again. I also don't want it brought here. Let's just insist on some simple justice." McTavish had to admit that Da was right, but how could one teach the Ornams a lesson and not hurt them. Brython said, "We can hurt them without killing them. We can do irreparable damage to their property, enough to make them move back to Dublin, where they belong. They stunk our house up. Why can't we burn their house down? We can do it when they're gone."

No one challenged Brython's idea; all that remained was for them to implement it and come up with a logical plan. Oleander devised a scheme. The family would go visit Craine in the hospital Saturday night and stay overnight, due to the impending surgery and be available for matching skin grafts. After hours the least matched would sneak out and place dynamite in the woods adjacent to the Ornam property. He would return, and the next least matched would sneak out and put several cans of gasoline at the cache, then return. The next in line would bring wood and tinder to start a small fire near the house. Early Sunday morning, the family would wait in the woods with binoculars to observe movement and to dig a hole to bury the equipment. They'd burn the shack while the family was at church.

After hearing this plan Tyndall stated if the Brits conscripted his family, they'd win their war in a week. No one was to tell Craine about it or the Constabulary would be torturing him about it from his hospital bed. Care had to be taken to cause it to appear that the earth over the hole had been untouched. Tyndall would handle this due to his prior experience as a landscaper. That Sunday the deed was done. If Jesse Ornam complained to the authorities, he would have to explain about the damage done to the Mikawbers' house and Craine. They had pictures of his face and arms, including the cuts and burns. No complaints were lodged with the authorities.

Craine was in a lot of pain and diverted himself from it by thinking what would happen if the shoe was on the other foot. He could picture skin being transplanted from Delphious' arse to his face with that picture of St. Patrick on his puss. Father Wrigley would probably beat the hell out of him for it. The nurses seemed to fall all over themselves because he knew how to fight back. They also knew his family also did when rumors flew around Belfast about the Ornams' house.

One girl in particular had a crush on him. She was Malkia. She was neither Catholic nor Protestant, but Jewish. She was freckle faced and had flaming red hair, brown eyes, shapely, long legs, bountiful breasts, and a shapely, juicy bottom. When she came in the room, and they were all alone, she would lie on him and hug him. She could tell in the obvious ways that he enjoyed her company. The same day he was in her embrace, his father and brothers came to visit him after their escapade at the Ornams' house. They were all in a jubilant mood and began to tease Craine about his getting beat up so he could enjoy Malkia's attentions. Tyndall asked what kind of wound he had to get to receive such attention. They found out her last name was Doleman and realized her religious affiliation. McTavish smiled and said, "At least ye won't be a tryin' to convert us. But we ain't learnin' any Hebrew. Ye'll probably have to sneak out of your Sabbath services to see us of a Friday night or a Saturday. We may even take you to church of a

Sunday, I'm warnin 'ye now. Your Da will probably beat the the Bejaysus out of you. This was not to be the last time McTavish made her laugh and blush at the same time.

Chapter 3

Britain tried different stunts, such as giving Protestant and Catholic trouble makers a choice between conscription and jail or the gallows. The next two years found Irish demands for home rule and Irishmen, elected to Parliament refusing to take their seats. Under an Irish leadership (de Valera) buildings were seized, and conscription was resisted. The Brits had to divert some of their western front soldiers to put down the rebellion in Dublin around the time that they were engaged with the Germans at the Somme. Also at around this time the tank was introduced as a weapon. This started Tyndall thinking that, perhaps Ireland, and his family, in particular, ought to learn some of the English strategy. They could use it to meet the Irish drive for freedom, and it could be used against them Lobsterbacks if they still wanted war with the Prots.

The British needed more manpower, and they knew that conscription wouldn't work with the Irish. They began releasing people from the jails, selling land back to owners at cheap rates, offering stipends to colleges for service. Some people were cooperative, but ulterior motives were present. Learning how to fight the Brits on their own terms made for a more formidable rebellion that had more of a chance of winning freedom from John Bull's yoke. Also stealing plane parts and sending them to Sinn Fein and Protestant militants was lucrative and gave the freedom fighters more sophisticated weaponry.

As far as Craine went, his scars healed beautifully. He and Malkia really began to hit it off well. His size and muscular frame kept other boys away from her. She spent Sundays with his family, and he spent Friday nights at her house to celebrate the Sabbath. Their family consisted of four girls and a big bruiser, Mendel, who was her older brother. He knew Craine from school and liked him because he took his side once when a group of anti-Semites tried to jump him. Her father, Moses, did not like a goy in his house, especially on Shabbos. However, the combination of Malkia's threat to leave home, his friendship with Mendel, and the fact that Craine was passing his push cart in downtown Belfast, while a bully was threatening to turn over the sheenie's cart. Craine picked the hater up by his neck and told him that if he didn't apologize to Mr. Doleman for the slur and threat immediately, today would be his last day on Earth. Needless to say the apology was delivered forthwith.

Craine began to learn Hebrew and Yiddish in bits and pieces and participated in the blessings and prayers. He began to be considered one of the family, as was Malkia in his house. He even began to attend Shul with them, and she began to attend Church with them. There was no talk of conversion or better or worse faiths. First Mendel, then Moses started to come over to the Mikawbers. Tyndall and Moses debated their theologies, while Mendel and McTavish arm wrestled, Malkia and Craine started to sneak away to be by themselves in the woods.

One spring Sunday, the sky was pure blue, and Malkia wanted to show Craine her favorite spot. They walked through the green of the north woods to a hill through which a clear brook ran. They followed the brook to its end, where it began to slope down into a valley in which daisies and marigolds bloomed with their rainbows of colors. The sight was breathtaking. Craine told his fair colleen that as beautiful as the field was, it did not hold a candle to her. She dropped his hand and drew him to her, then she circled her arms around his neck. He drew her lips to his and kissed her, very gently. She drew his mouth to her and kissed him with all the passion she had within her. She pressed her breasts against him and could feel him begin to swell. Craine began to unbutton her blouse and loosen her undergarments. She began to unfasten his belt and felt his tumescence. She pulled him down to the ground in the grass and begged him to enter her. He brought his mouth to her breast and said it was like the goblet of wine that David drew from the royal cup of Israel. She moaned at his words and pleaded to be taken. They began to quiver and rock together.

Craine began to moan, "My sweet Malkia you are the bliss of the Rose of Sharon." And they reached their peak and lay with each other.

Suddenly Craine felt a slap across the back of his head. He looked up, startled and saw Moses' backhand and his father, along with Mendel. Their expressions were not pleasant. Moses addressed his daughter sternly. "You are no longer of my house. You have had carnal knowledge of a gentile and are unwed. I pray that this act does not destroy our friendship, Tyndall." Tyndall answered that it would not and that he would take Malkia in until the couple made other plans.

In the next week, both a Rabbi and the family reverend of the Mikawbers officiated over their wedding, and Moses sat Chiveh for his daughter. She was not allowed in her father's house again. She was not pregnant. Moses was friendly with the family, as was Mendel, but they vowed that they'd never again acknowledge the presence of Malkia.

Craine knew that though his family loved them both dearly, economics dictated that their stay would be temporary. Craine was only fifteen, but he was huge for his age and grew a mustache to look older. Malkia did not want to be separated from him and knew that he had been talking about wanting to learn how to fly. They had heard about Lafayette Escadrille, in which Frenchmen and Americans that felt they had to get into the war against Germany had formed a squadron to fight as a unit until America entered the war.

Although the Protestants wanted to enjoy British protection because of the Catholic threat to them, the Mikawbers were different. Tyndall and his family believed if one put his trust in others, it had a price. They wanted home rule and also wanted Sinn Fein to know that they were responsible to uphold the writings that granted religious and civil liberty to all Irishmen. In keeping with this philosophy, Craine and Malkia agreed to send plans and parts of the aeroplanes home to their Da.

They left after a short honeymoon, for Bar-le-Duc where Lafayette Escadrille was based. The commanders were Dr. Edmund L. Gros and Norman Prince. Cdr. Prince made a comment about this not being a woman's war, and Craine stepped up and told the commander that his wife was not an ordinary woman. He retorted with, "She damn well better not be." He proceeded to ask them how much experience they had with flying. When they admitted that they had none, he curtly stated that they would receive their first lesson in fifteen minutes and would be expected to learn how to fly, master the weapons and parts of the plane, know how to land, in six weeks, and to toughen their bodies by exercises and learning how to take a fall at the same time. If they could not do this, they would be sent to the infantry or go home and blow their noses. By the dictates of the times, he was tougher on Malkia until she proved she was tougher than he was. He touched her inappropriately while teaching her how to break a choke hold, and she touched him inappropriately with her foot, a smack to his jaw while he bent over, and banging his head on a rock as he fell. Craine was busy learning himself and did not see the event. When he found out that night, he marched over to his tent and clobbered the commander so that he flew across the room and beat him bloody with a table leg he broke off the officer's table. Unbelievably, they had respect and friendship for each other throughout the war after this.

They had mastered what they had to do in two weeks, instead of six. By the time July came around they got to prove themselves at Verdun. This battle was a 10 month ordeal with Germany trying to secure the western front and France trying not to let them pass.

Under the command of Petain, the bodies were scattered on the ground with more density than a typical field of wheat. Movement was not successful or strategically advantageous for either side; in the end 970,000 men lay dead for nothing. To defend the area, the air had to be cleared. Malkia hovered behind her husband like a mother bear and sent three Huns crashing to the ground. Craine found her trapped by three Fokker planes. He had one of them in his sights and blasted him into the Kaiser's mustache. She shot down the one to the side of her, and he led the one in front of her off and lured him to crash into a tree and explode. As he flew off, he tipped his plane at an angle to say goodbye.

The next cheery opportunity to demonstrate air prowess came at a river that provided a potential breakthrough point for the British army, the Somme. The motivating factor for this battle was a week long artillery bombardment. The Germans had merely to get out of their dugouts and destroy the oncoming waves of British soldiers. As a result England lost 57,470 men. The artillery had to be stopped. Britain needed help in getting out of the way of the guns to get across the river. Lafayette Escadrille devised a strategy to send two bombers to the river with 10 fighters to each bomber. Craine was in a two seater with a Frenchie, named Rodin La Monde. They were holding their own weight, keeping the fighters off of the bomber, when a wolf pack of German planes came out of the clouds. They were led by their own greed into a trap and knew it. They tried to blast their way out of the deadly circle any way they could. They could not get above the Bosches because every time they tried, a German would go up with them. Craine started to climb then quickly descended and nailed the Boche on the bottom, while Rodin threw a grenade on the one above. The flames broke up the circle, and the others could be taken one at a time.

On the way back to base, they followed the bomber, and the tail caught fire. Craine guided the plane to the tail gunner's cockpit, and Rodin stretched and instructed the machine gunner to stretch out and reach out for his arms so that he could be pulled aboard their plane. The gunner did so. When the gunner was pulled to the fighter plane, the helmet came off, revealing the long hair of Malkia. Everyone, but her had left the plane, and it crashed onto the German artillery below. The boys were cheered by the rest of the squad and taken out for beers that night. Malkia was with them and saw a French waitress try to make a pass at Craine. Before she could react, Rodin drew her attention away by playing footsies with her after she sat down at their table. After this, the three of them became inseparable.

Craine and Malkia built a close knit relationship with each other. In their letters, Malkia always asked about her father only to receive silence and an answer from Tyndall. Her brother wanted to break the silence, but he was warned by his father that he would be similarly expelled from the family and shunned if he tried it. However, the two of them were true to their word and sent drawn plans of technical features of French, American, German, British planes, cannons, rifles, and the newly developed tank home to Da. They smuggled them out of the country in loaves of French bread, in the linings of sexy ladies

13

nightwear, under the labels of French wine bottles, and in the linings of the cheapest paintings they could afford at the Louvre. This caused them problems after the war.

After the third battle of Ypre, the couple found that Malkia was pregnant. The Americans were about to enter the war and to dissolve Lafayette Escadrille. Saying goodbye to Rodin and the two commanders was hard, and they vowed to keep in touch.

Their homecoming was one of love and happiness. Moses could not show affection for his intransigent daughter. However, he did allow Mendel to run to her and give her a hug and a kiss, while tears came to his eyes, and he blew his nose into a red and white handkerchief which he had found in a field.

Moses could not ignore his daughter. He felt too much love for her. Besides, if God was indeed a loving God, He could not expect him to turn on his flesh and blood for marrying outside of the religion. He felt that the rejection was a repugnant and hypocritical act. Therefore, he reconciled with Malkia and Craine. He and Mendel joined Craine and the Mikawbers in building a house on a peripheral corner of Tyndall's land. However, it was on the point closest to the Ornams' property, and they remembered the burning of their home. Yet they did not remember that Tyndall wanted to spare human life, despite the lust for retaliation and that they had used fire first and put Craine in the hospital.

The house was built in 3 weeks. The couple was very happy and close to their families, which were rapidly blending into one family. They held Shabbos at the Dolemans and Sundays at the Mikawbers. On Shabbos, Malkia was tired and wanted to stay at home and sleep. Craine put his ear and face to her belly to feel the baby and to hear its kicking. He kissed his wife goodbye and went to join his family at the Dolemans'

The Ornams picked this time to be lurking in the bushes with their incendiary equipment. Malkia just finished snuggling up to the warmth of her husband's earlier presence and dozing off. She smelled kerosene and jumped out of bed suddenly. She saw flames. The door was barred by boulders placed against it. She couldn't open the window and had to break it to get out through the broken glass.

Four hours later her family found her lying unconscious and bleeding. Tyndall rushed to get the wagon ready, and they got her to the hospital. She lived, and so did the baby, by a miracle. Craine was in a rage and vowed revenge. His fathers did not talk him out of it. Tyndall reported the attempt to the constable and went personally to the Ornams' with Malkia, who identified Jesse, having seen him through the window. The constable was a Sinn Feiner and arranged an escape for Jesse from the jail in which he was being held for trial. He also happened to have tickets to New Zealand available for him. Craine found out about it and cornered the officer at his rounds at midnight so that he could not be seen at night. He was smart enough to wear black clothes and did not talk, for fear his voice would be recognized. He did not tell his family about this, and they did not know his whereabouts. He came up behind the constable, put him in a headlock, picked him up, and threw him in a garbage can. He then rolled the garbage can into a field where people walked their dogs and dumped a container of feces he accumulated throughout the day into the can. The exhausted constable fell asleep in the can and awoke next morning to an unusual aroma about himself. He was able to figure out what had happened, but he did not have any proof of who the culprit was although he knew who the family was.

Chapter 4

Two months later Malkia had a 26 inch boy of 12 lbs. He was named Patrick Tyndall Moses Mikawber. She had to lock Craine out of their house because he kept lining up behind his son to be breast fed and wouldn't adhere to the six week period of abstinence post pregnancy. He began to spend time with the aeroplane his father and brothers had built from his directions and shipment of stolen parts. He wanted to fly by the Ornams and strafe their house, but he knew that the constable was still angry about being put in a garbage can full of feces and knew who did it. He observed that he had not forgotten the rockets and machine guns and reassured himself that a day would come.

The time was coming for Pat's bris, and he had to go to shul with the Dolemans and his family. Afterwards they all went out to a restaurant, and Mendel suggested that he leave Pat's foreskin as a tip for the waitress. Malkia kicked him under the table. She had the sweetest grin on her face when she did it. Brython started laughing, and everyone else joined in.

At one site there was no laughter going on. Jesse Ornam did not like the fact that the house was rebuilt and that Malkia and the baby survived. Though St. Pat was scraped off Delphious' arse, he still had scars on his face where he was cut. The Mikawbers had to pay for that, as well as Craine's betraying his nation and fighting in the Brits' war. He never considered that Tyndall and his family wanted freedom from Britain as much as he did. Jesse also did not like the idea of Craine not converting to the right way to approach God, where he would've stood before his maker with a righteous soul. Instead, he gave himself to the Christ killer Jews. He spit on the ground when this crossed his mind. Too bad that his sheenie wife made it and brought another one of their unholy mess into the world. Next time his family would take them both off of the earth. They probably were the part of England that sucked the land and money out of Ireland.

Jesse was not silent about his rage, and Delphious helped spread his sick hate throughout the family. Their discussions at the dinner table became a forum for echoing the senseless anger that propelled them into violent thoughts. This was not enough for the dynamic duo of hatred, but they became loud and irrational at Sinn Fein meetings. The infection was spreading. After a couple months a plan was conceived. The Eastern Europeans made the Jews stay in their place. They kept them out of public office, kept them away from money, and made them pollute their own sections of towns and cities. Maybe Ireland ought to take up the cause of creating a Christian state.

Weapons and incendiary devices were cached, manufactured on the sly, cleaned, oiled, and stocked with ammo by the Ornam's for two months. The buildup was extended to the Sinn Fein, and a considerable supply was being hoarded for the time of reckoning. This was not between the Ornams and Mikawbers, but directed towards getting England out of Ireland, along with their Protestant stooges. No attention was paid to the idea that the family was looking for the same freedom for their native land that Sinn Fein was, as were the small number of Jews that were in Eire. Prejudice and the small mindedness that comes from escalated anger seemed to be the dominant modes of thought of the day. The escalation that followed was to have devastating consequences.

The cache of weaponry was to begin the blast for Irish independence that lasted from 1919 to 1922 when a patchwork quilt of peace was to be knit between the two nations later to emerge as the terrorist acts of the militant Protestants, the militant Catholic followers that coined the phrase "Erin go Bragh," as their voice of terror that spanned church attacks, attacks on innocent children and families, incarceration, hangings, and retaliation by starvation diets. Now the bloodletting would gain full expression.

The Ornam and other Sinn Fein families began to hold practice drills in the hand to hand combat that had punctuated the trench warfare of the "War to end all wars." Of course the Prots saw what was coming and began to hold their own drills. The first attack assumed the shape of a pogrom. The Dolemans were attacked, and the Mikawbers joined in the defense of their kinsmen. The plane was a secret weapon and had not been unleashed, but this was to happen shortly. The house was fired, and little Pat and Malkia were hidden in a locker of the basement that covered a tunnel out to the woods with a clear line to the constable's office. Jesse was about to use his tickets to New Zealand to get out of Ireland for good, but he stayed long enough to get a final lick at his foes.

He was a part of the raid on the Doleman house and had observed the point where the tunnel ended. He met Malkia and Pat at the exit and shot them both. Then he ran to keep his appointment with his boat, which turned out to be his appointment with destiny. For Craine went to the hidden hangar, started the plane, made sure it was loaded, and sunk the ship right after Jesse had boarded. He then flew back to the Dolemans' and strafed the pogrom in front of their house while the defenders came out of their barricade and made short shrift of the bullies. Tyndall was able to get Malkia and Pat to the hospital. Pat was able to survive, but his mother did not make it. Not one Ornam came forth to express sorrow.

Craine's expression was not of sorrow. He moved the plane to a new hideout because after his next episode, he knew he'd have to leave the country. He had already gotten rid of the head of the garbage family; he just had to bide his time, but he had to make plans for Pat. At the next family meeting, he told Da and the others: "Lads, I'm demanding an eye for an eye for Malkia. I know I took Jesse out, and probably a lot of innocent people with him. You know what that makes me. If I didn't harm another soul, I'd hang for what I did. To prevent a family feud that would tear us apart too, I have to take out the rest of them. I'd like nothing better than to stay here and throw off the British yoke, but my staying would put you in danger. I know what I'm going to do, and then I'll be gone. My only question is: Do I leave me Patrick under your care, or do I take him with me, so he knows his Da?" There were tears in all the Mikawber eyes, especially Tyndall. As the head of the house he addressed the issue. "Me son, a bairn has to know his Da. There's no mother to sing his praises. Ye'll be held within our memories and our hearts, as well as the Dolemans for loving their daughter, bringing them a son, and stopping the first pogrom our village has ever experienced. May God bless you and our Patrick, and bring you back to us." With that they all cried. The scene was repeated before the Dolemans that Shabbos. The sorrow and the tears flowed from both families that had become and would remain one.

On Monday, Craine bundled up Pattie with resolve in his heart and tears centered in the same organ and took the plane to the Ornam's home. They were all leaving for work. He bombed their wagon with them all in it, including the lady of the house. With them all scattered over Belfast he set his sites for Boston, Massachusetts where he could lose himself in the big Irish population.

Chapter 5

The years flew by swiftly. Pattie was five years old, and Craine kept in weekly contact with his family. The youngster kept in touch with his family in the old country and his Jewish family. He was kept busy with Hebrew lessons, Yiddish lessons, and Erse poetry by virtue of the efforts of his Da and Grand Da who wrote him in the Gaelic and Celtic tongues. He showed an adeptness for languages, the history of his peoples (Jewish, Irish, and the ways of the Auld Orange). He was intrigued with knowing how things were put together and how processes worked. Craine worked as a trucker and came in contact with all different types of people. With no pubs in America and with passage of the Volstead Act, Craine began to look at the art of rum running across the Canadian border. However, he found that both Italian and Irish gangs were fighting for control of this market, and the fights got pretty nasty. Boston was not the least expensive community to raise a boy, and Craine needed more income than what a truck driver could earn.

On one of his treks by truck, he met Georgie "Bugs" Moran, while at a Canadian bar, they talked about the war between the Italians and the Irish, wars over control of alcohol, prostitution, gambling. They were making money hand over fist, despite the killings, wars, cops on the take and politicians in their pockets. He began to get familiar with names, such as Al Capone, Johnnie Torrio, Big Jim Colosemo, and, last, but not least, Dinty O'Banion. Craine liked what he heard about him. He was a Lobsterback, but he could be friends with a Jew (Hymie Weiss). He took care of the Irish in Chicago and could give the impression of working with Italians and make sure that the profits went into Irish pockets. He stole Italian south side businesses and incomes from people with whom he worked and made sure that the

Irish North side saw the profits. He had a beautiful tenor voice and ran the best flower shop in Chicago, as a front. The concept of front was new to Craine. He was used to the idea that a man knew where he stood. It was news that he only had to inspire fear when he intended to act fearfully. The aspect of being polite and appearing gentle while slipping it to someone else was an American nuance that seemed to go a long way. Obviously more could be accomplished with a little honey instead of a lot of vinegar.

Craine already knew that Dinty was involved with the trade unions in the form of combating the employers' use of scabs and sluggers to break up attempts to start unions. Ironically he had planned to use Louisville Sluggers to hit a couple homeruns. He remembered McTavish giving some Lobsterback a black eye for mouthing a bunch of anti union garbage and chuckled on the way into Chicago; Bugsy had accompanied him on the trip to deliver a load of lumber to a yard near the site of a potential strike. A tarpaulin was put over the truck to hide the company name. At a prearranged meeting with Dinty, 32 bats were supplied to 32 workers, and a couple machine gunners were in the back of the truck with them to look out for Pinkerton men.

Craine had a lot of time to think about what he was planning. Drivers had a lot of time to themselves on the road. The boss gave the signal for the strikebreakers to move in, and the Pinkerton men were alerted. He chuckled to himself when he contemplated what those suckers were in for; union indeed. The big bruisers came with the fruit and eggs they'd throw at socialist suckers, the union agitators and maybe get their chance to beat the hell out of the punks. A speaker brought a self made podium to speak to the workers and started in about the inequitable distribution of income to profits, while workers sustained injuries after long hours on the assembly line, could not spend time with their sons, as a father wanted to do because of these hours and the demand to keep producing. The first response was to throw eggs at the speaker. The second was for the bruisers to advance on the listeners, tell the bum to get out of there, and to start to pick up listeners, and throw them around a little, even throwing them on the ground and kicking their ribs. As some of the men being kicked began to grab at the kicking legs, Pinkerton men advanced on them. The progress, witnessed by the laughing boss, was interrupted by a truck moving closer to the melee. The vehicle stopped; the doors opened, and the sound of machine gun fire was heard. The Pinkerton men were no more. Men with ball bats swarmed out of the back. The bruisers that wanted to be free of being part of the regime to beat Babe Ruth's record made it their business to run home. By Monday, the union contract was signed. After a couple such slugfests, Chicago was on the road to become a union town. Bugsy and Craine split $50,000. It was good to be a trucker. Craine sent $10,000 home to Da and Moses.

The relationship with Dinty was profitable but short lived. In 1924, Al Capone and Johnny Torrio got sick of the glib flower peddler shaking their hands with one hand and stealing from them with the other. He was shot to death in the middle of a handshake.

Craine did not like to leave Pattie alone and hired a babysitter until he was about 12 years old. He kept his plans to himself and was able to hide a lot from his son. He also did not let Bugs or anyone else know that he had a son because he didn't want him to be vulnerable to any retaliatory moves from any gangsters. Pattie grew into Patrick, who suspected some of his father's activities, but who also knew enough to not ask any questions. He did not condemn his fathers' moves because he had memories about what motivated them. He remembered a shooting incident from a plane, just before he and Da had left Ireland, in which a whole bunch of people were blown up. These people were somehow connected with his mother's death. Da was always, always gentle when he came home before and after that day. But the look he had in his eyes the day he shot down that wagon was terrifying to Patrick.

The trips to Chicago were becoming more frequent, and Craine was beginning to become well known. He suggested to Bugs that, perhaps, they should open up other markets in other areas. People that were beginning to rise in power in the Mafia, as the Italian gangs were beginning to be known, under Al Capone, since Johnny Torrio had vacated his position began to single out Craine for eliminating rivalry. He did not like this for two reasons. He did not like becoming a killer, and he did not like the idea of Eliot Ness becoming aware of him. Craine found him to be a dogged enemy of lawbreakers, who believed in an eye for an eye. He did not want to be one of his targets.

When he met with Bugs, he suggested getting involved with the Purple Gang, from Detroit, where an automobile industry was flourishing, and where automobile producers did not want unions cutting into their profit margins. He also thought the Americans would get sick of prohibition and vote it out of legality. He did not like prostitution because of how it demeaned the soul of a woman. He could remember the effects of nerve gas during the war and felt drugs would reduce a human being to a mass of blubbering jelly. The growing mass of government control of lives, evidenced by the legislative and executive use of power was destroying humanity enough. In years to come, the meaning of freedom and of responsibility would become obscured, if not destroyed. Craine reasoned that he didn't want to assist the process by creating a nation of slobbering weaklings with drugs. This is the way that crime was going, the way of business, with its brutality and impersonality. Though he knew he entered a world of evil, and he had entered it voluntarily, he entered it to protect himself and his family, not to sin against God's Law for his own greed.

Two major events occurred, that brought Bugs around to Craine's way of thinking: St. Valentine's Day Massacre and the arrest of Al Capone. On Feb-14-1929, 5 men walked into S.M.C. Cartage Co. where six members of the Moran gang were meeting, and a mechanic was working on a car. Three men were dressed as policemen, and two were in street clothes. They ordered the seven men to line up against the wall and shot them down then walked out with the men in street clothes acting as if they were apprehended gangsters. George Moran was supposed to be one of the men shot, but he wasn't there. The men were Capone hirelings. To dissociate himself from the murders, Capone went for a vacation at this home in Miami, Florida. The second event was a triumph for Eliot Ness. In 1931, Al Capone was sentenced to eleven years incarceration at a federal prison for income tax evasion. His gang leadership was taken over by Frank Nitty. After this Bugs and Craine considered moving their activities to other cities and began to move into legitimate areas of endeavor.

Patrick never forgot about the Jewish, Irish mixture in his heritage.

He learned Hebrew, Yiddish, and some of the Gaelic/Erse poetry in his background. To help hone his skills, he wrote to Grand Da in Gaelic and to Moses in Yiddish. He also prepared for his Bar Mitzvah. Craine sent money to Da and Moses to make the trip over. This meant a temporary break from his avocation.

The reunion was one of joy and laughter. Mendel tried to arm wrestle Pat and found himself lacking. But he and Craine held themselves at the same standstill. At the moment of manhood, Pat spoke about the world in which culture and love of mankind for each of its disparate elements was rapidly being replaced by love of the dollar, no matter how its ability to purchase the goods that were translated to mean the love that it was replacing. He spoke of the ideals for which his family, for which his entire family, both Jewish and Irish had spent their blood. He spoke of a war that was to end all wars and left the world with seething hate, suppression of minorities, creation of minorities to sustain the materialism, crookedness, and closed the door to understanding the small, kicked around little guy. He said that these things would blow up, and that a more devastating war would ensue. At the end of his speech, Tyndall and Da's brothers stood and cheered; Moses stood with them. There were tears of pride in his eyes, but no red and white handkerchief found in a field. From this day forth, Craine, Moses, Tyndall and the rest referred to him as Patrick because today he became a man.

Chapter 6

The year 1930 marked Patrick's emerging manhood, Craine's questioning his involvement with the criminal elements in America and Ireland, emigration of the Mikawber/Doleman clan to Boston, then to Williamsburg, Virginia. It was also a time when Craine found the capacity to love a woman again. It was also a time when men, who could not reconcile the loss of this new God, money, and began to see what people had to do to survive in reality.

After Patrick's Bar Mitzvah, the whole clan went for a trip to Williamsburg for a gift to the young man. They saw how colonists worked, lived, ate, and became motivated to love their country. While participating in a mock battle of the Revolutionary War, Moses got carried away to the streets of Warsaw and Belfast fighting anti-Semites and British landlords at the same time. He whooped and hollered to Mendel, Tyndall, and anyone in earshot that he shot a Brit Redcoat in the arse so many times, and he wouldn't drop; he got sick of it and clobbered him with the rifle butt. You betcha the bastid fell that time. Tyndall had to tell him it was only a game and not a war. War, he did not need to fight anymore because he lived in a free country. Moses' last words were, "By God, if it's that free, I'll move here, and the hell with Boston. I like fights, but I never saw a man that could take ten bullets in the arse and keep standing. "Apparently he never learned what the concept of a blank bullet meant. Since he was so dead set on moving there, Tyndall and the rest of the Mikawbers joined him.

Craine could see that Patrick was more interested in being with his friends than in family outings by the way he was eyeing some of the teenaged females involved in the mock battles, bread making, flag sewing, and cooking activities. He also was excited about engaging in a pickup baseball game with some of the young men of the community. He decided to pursue some of his own interests, as he watched a rather interesting lady bend over to wipe a smudge off of her shoe. He smirked at her and said it would be less interesting to him, but kinder to her if she let him wipe it off for her. She stood up all startled and blushing to tell him to mind his own business and to take his rude brogue back to Dublintown, or wherever he came from. He laughed and said Dublin wouldn't exactly appreciate his presence; he further indicated he'd take her on in a game of darts at any pub in Belfast. At this, her anger subsided, and she laughed. She told him that she was looking for a job as a mock nurse in the mock battle. He hired her for the job. She was so excited that she didn't ask if he worked there. She asked when she could start, and he said he didn't know, but he'd ask the personnel manager if she gave him her name. Before she could get all angered again, he asked if she'd give him and his family a tour followed by the best Irish dinner she ever ate. Her name was Molly Karhill. The anger that started in her soul was changed to laughter by the antics of Tyndall, Moses, Mendel, the rest of the Mikawber/Doleman clan, and last, but not least, Craine. What he expected to be the worst smack in the kisser turned out to be the nicest kiss he ever got.

There were picnics in the park and swimming at the beaches in Virginia, New England, Coney Island, trips on the Freedom Trail, trips to presidents' homes, to museums. Molly accompanied Patrick to Hebrew classes and learned to read Scholem Aleichem in Yiddish. She also learned to read the poetry of the old Gaelic writers from the Protestant minister and some of the priests. He even introduced her to Bugs Moran, who was struggling, in vain to keep his empire from crumbling to dust. She was aware of his notoriety, but she enjoyed him as a person from it. Craine felt the pangs of guilt about considering another woman to take the place of Malkia until he had a talk with Patrick about it. Pat said that his leaving home was but a few years off, and though he loved him and Grand Da and Da Moses, he'd be building his own life. He said he also found Molly fun and loveable.

The following weekend, Craine took Molly to a cave in the Berkshire Mountains. She thought the woods were romantic and groaned as they ascended the peaks to the cave. She was awed by the point where a stalactite merged with a stalagmite. A tear came to Craine's eye as he described what the merger meant to him. It meant that the righteous anger of God was joined with the unrighteous greed and lust for power that Satan sought and that Mankind would be in an eternal conflict over which could be applied to do the most good. Molly startled him with a question that asked why doing good had to be attached to anger. Couldn't loving one's self and one's fellow man be a guide for seeking the good in life?

Craine considered this proposition and tried to annex this thought to his belief that he had to fight for everything he got. Molly told him the story of the friendship that developed between a lion and a mouse when the mouse pulled the thorn from the lion's foot, and how Joseph earned the reputation of being skilled at dream interpretation by interpreting a fellow prisoner's dream and having this passed on to Pharaoh. That night they swam in the hotel pool, and she divested herself of her suit and swam into his arms and kissed him tenderly. He carried her to their room by using the elevator and laid her gently on the bed. They enjoyed the rest of the night making love.

As Craine had grown up in the violence of the "War to end all wars" and the violence all around him, Patrick had to grow up around men building themselves up at the expense of others to the extent of creating a disparity in the income available to owners and producers. Sympathy for the little guy with the guts to work his way to the top has been a cornerstone of American philosophy. When Clyde Barrow made the statement, "We rob banks," it won him a name amongst many impoverished small time dust bowl farmers. When the monied classes found themselves reaching into empty pockets after the stock market crash, they began to jump out of windows. Those that survived did so because they found that two parties have to cling together to fight their way through a mechanical, impersonal world, composed of people who don't care about others. "By the sweat of your brow, shall you earn your bread." Men like Craine and Bugs Moran were, through the consequences they were suffering, being shown that there are alternatives to getting ahead by stepping over a corpse.

In addition to the philosophical contrasts stimulated by the meeting of the stalactite and stalagmite, Craine had an ulterior motive: He wanted to take Molly flying. He showed her the plane, explained the history of its building, and uses, and asked her if she wanted the freedom and beauty of the air God had made for them. He took her up in the sky, where the clouds were like vapors of smoke, and the land looked like little squares of green and bustling ants along the highways. She was utterly fascinated by the change in view she saw and was also just as intrigued by being able to get away from the smallness of life, as illustrated by the ease by which a living being could have the life snuffed out of him/her. Viewing the vastness of the sky/universe renewed her faith in the concept of a power beyond Man, whose plan we cannot fully comprehend.

The hopes of Patrick and Tyndall seemed to hinge together in the hope that Craine could see some good in life. He did not know his mother very well since most of her life was spent trying to remove herself from the earthly existence that bound her pain wracked life to her husband and children. Craine knew the tearful emptiness his father had felt and wondered how he had the strength to love him, as he did. Life was further complicated by the practice of fighting to preserve who you were. His concept was beginning to be shaped into what can we build ourselves to be by loving one another, despite the obstacles in our way.

Section II

Rodin La Monde

Cry Heaven, Cry Hell

Chapter 1

Before describing the battle that scarred a family name for centuries, I would like to paint a picture of what I saw over two hundred years later at a park site, which was erected on the battlefield that had ended a war. I saw greenery that was divided by bicycle paths, upon which I had attempted to ride a rented bike and had a flat tire. For the first time in my life, I saw a beaver. These sights were not conducive to understanding that British influence and not French influence would prevail in Canada. Yet Quebec remained an area where French influence was heavily felt. Is the argument that might makes right, indeed a truism, or does the suppression of minorities act to create people that are frozen in the dialectic of revenge, as were Craine Mikawber and Rodin La Monde.

The physical date of Rodin's birth was 07-14-1887. However, historically he was born on 09-13-1759. On this date a battle was fought on the western edge of the wall of Quebec. It marked the date of the defeat of the French army by the British army and navy. Both opposing commanders lost their lives, and the entire battle took an hour after Britain had laid siege to the city for three months. The point of the battle was to see who had the right to exploit the Native American, as their colonizer.

Among the French soldiers were militiamen, who were not completely trained. They had not mastered maneuverability skills so that they could fire and reload rapidly enough to keep up a consistent pattern of concentrated fire. Among these was an ill prepared battalion under Charles Michel de Langlade. He was part French and part Odawa (later Ottawa) Indian. He led a battalion of Odawa under the tribal leadership of Lonely Otter. When the consistency of the firing pattern fell to the wayside, a French officer verbally assaulted Lonely

Otter then cut his ear off with a sword. He subsequently led his men into a slaughter because he couldn't hear from what direction the firing of the enemy came. The descendants of this man spoke about the incident from one generation to the next, including men, thought of as French citizens. These were the people of Rodin's family. And the hatred was passed on.

Rodin decided to be systematic about his endeavor. He would operate in the colonies in which France was the most hated and the weakest in its stature. He started out by becoming conversant with the historical and cultural patterns.

After the defeat of Napoleon in 1815 until the restoration of the monarchy in 1830, France became a weakened state. There was a surplus of idle soldiers, an excess of artillery that was not being used. With greedy eyes the nation looked to Africa and Asia where armies were not strong because they had other ideas besides warfare on their minds. The Algerian dey was weak, and this "Cradle of Democracy" used an insult to their consul as an excuse, first to blockade Algiers for three years then launched a military expedition against the city. They raped women, desecrated mosques, looted the treasury. The struggle became long and violent, with the French exterminating one third of the population. Having had the temerity to make Algeria a part of France allowed them to export not only settlers from their own land, but also Spain, Italy, and Malta to take the land from the native farmers and cultivate it. The result was the literacy and educational upscaling of Algerians fell. The foreign migrants were granted full French citizenship, while native Algerian Muslims didn't even have the right to vote in their own native land. In 1954 a War of Independence was declared. It took almost a decade for France to defeat The National Liberation Front, and a plebiscite was held which finally resulted in independence.

Even the Romans knew of Vietnam, as far as 166 B.C. The Portuguese and Dutch became involved in the 1500's, backing rival families in the North and South. In 1784 a French Bishop intervened on behalf of the Southern family in return for concessions to France. The assistance was interrupted by the French Revolution and taken up after that. The attempts to impose Catholicism served as a focus to the

Confucian population to resist Westernization. This was the excuse that France needed to invade the country. Throughout the 19th century the French colonized both the North and South with many resistance movements that led only to defeat of the Vietnamese. In the quest for modernization to build an army that could throw out the foreigners, exposure to Marxism occurred. In 1941, Ho Chi Minh became leader of the Viet Minh, a front to fight for Vietnamese independence. It was dominated by Vietnamese communists. Vietnam had been exploited by the Japanese during WWII. After the war the Viet Minh launched a revolution to seize the offices of government. France tried to re-establish their rule, but Ho Chi Minh received aid from communist China. War broke out in 1947 and lasted until the battle of Dien Bien Phu, in 1954. The modernly weaponed French underestimated the ability of the Viet Minh to move heavy artillery over the mountains and surrendered to them in this famous battle, while U.S. advisers watched the other "Cradle of Liberty" flounder.

One of the terms of the Geneva Agreement stated that Vietnam would be divided into two countries: North and South Vietnam. The South was ruled by a strong anti-communist, Ngo Dinh Diem. He urged the United States to back his counter revolutionary force against the communist North. Communists, Buddhists, and students in the South all joined to oppose his dictatorial rule. A National Liberation Front arose to throw Diem out. The U.S.A. was pressured to send military advisors. In 1964, an American ship was sunk in the Bay of Tonkin. The North was attacked by the air. This launched the Vietnamese War, in which the U.S.A. was evacuated from Vietnam.

Rodin absorbed these facts and their implications for his family war against the French Empire. In Algeria, he became an agitator and a trainer for guerilla soldiers in the cities and rural areas. He backed socialist movements to draw the Algerian attention to the inequities of natives of a country being denied educational opportunities or to benefit from new agricultural techniques because a foreigner had moved in their land to benefit her own lackeys and to deny them the fruits of their own labor. Along with the attacks on the thinking that questioned what benefit France had brought to this nation, came training programs. Stolen weapons were diagrammed and assembled and re-assembled; the discipline to face interrogators and tell them lies to mislead them was integrated into their personhood. The points of vulnerability on the body were practiced until they became rote; the most vulnerable point of a tank was learned. Assembly of machine guns, rocket launchers, howitzers was learned in detail so that they could be rapidly assembled or destroyed. Where modern weapons were not available, use of what was there was adapted to defense and offense.

The most difficult skill that Rodin had to learn was non-identity. When blocks of people had learned the abilities he taught them or when French victory seemed imminent, he had to be able to disappear. The people whom he taught, and for whom he agitated were not to know his name or face. Many times he wore a disguise. Sometimes he led boycotts or demonstrations, then he had to disappear on a rooftop or in the sea. The important impact was that he start the anger flowing and disappear at the point of the highest escalation.

He joined the French Foreign Legion after the war and played both ends against the middle in Algeria. He would attack the Berber villages during the day, participate in the raping, pillaging and destruction. At night, he'd dress as an Arab woman named Rebaza and complain to the men about her sons starving because all the land was given to foreigners to cultivate while the natives were left without land, or she would lament about her sons not being educated for anything, but to be cannon fodder for the French wars. Then Hitler invaded France. This was his chance to score points as a French hero and undermine her at the same time.

Much later, at Dien Bien Phu, he had to play a dual role and move between Viet Minh, as a Russian advisor and Frenchmen shouting misconstrued orders to the soldiers. To get from one side to the other, he had to build a tunnel within a tunnel and negotiate it at a rapid speed as the battle progressed. By the time the Americans took over the war, he was long gone. He brought back the principle that the Japanese had used of operating through tunnels, in case the Vietnamese were not familiar with it, which they evidently were.

Chapter 2

Having established rapport with the Vichy government and the Underground during the war, Rodin was able to operate with a free reign. Because of this he was able to affect a rescue that was based on a connection with his past. A B-17 bomber was sent to blow up a munitions plant that was sending rockets across the channel from the Danish peninsula. It was intercepted by a squad of Messerschmitts and shot down. There were two survivors that had to outrace German troops. Suddenly shots rang out ahead of the crewmen. The Germans lay dead behind them. Rodin stepped out of the bushes and demanded to know who the survivors were. The first one answered, "I am Lieutenant Patrick Mikawber, of the U.S. Army Air Force, and this is Sergeant Corlando Moran, of the same. Rodin had thought that this first one looked familiar. He told him that he knew his father and mother from Lafayette Escadrille. He recounted some of their adventures, and Pat updated him on what had happened to his family and their emigration. He did not talk about his father's escapades, just mentioned that he had started out as a truck driver and had started his own company (which actually happened).

He wanted to accomplish his mission. The Underground unit and the two flyers planned to disguise them as workers in the plant wearing face masks in the likenesses of two Underground that actually worked there. They sneaked dynamite and fusing in their lunch pails and planted it at various sites in the plant. Corlando almost got them caught when he tried to look up the skirt of a female employee that had bent over to pick up a dropped part. They tied the fusing to the ends of the dynamite sticks, then knotted all the sticks together. When they got out, they tied a knot to another length of fusing and tied this length to the detonator. When the plunger was pushed, the explosion rocked the village, and whatever employees could get out barged through the door. Corlando saw the girl at whom he peeked, run out; he ran up to her and kissed her. After the war, he went back and started a relationship with her.

Now the task was to get the flyers out of the country. They were smuggled out in a boatload of llamas, aardvarks, and anteaters bound for an Amsterdam zoo. After this, they were transported to the Cliffs of Dover at the bottom of a garbage scow. Pat wrote his father and Molly about this adventure and added greetings from Rodin.

Rodin was always serious about his dual role. However, he enjoyed the opposite sex and had an opportunity to meet a woman that thought the war was absolutely the most stupid endeavor entered upon by mankind because she felt that men's egos were not worth the slaughter in which they were engaged. She also did not approve of the hypocrisy of speaking about protecting freedom and creating a minority of the citizens of the indigenous peoples of the nations they colonized. Her name was Liana Dobrovna, and she worked as a dancer in a local bar. She approached him to buy her a drink, but a Nazi officer wanted her attention and pulled her away from him. He also began to twist her arm. Rodin began to sing "Deutschland, Deutschland Uber Alles" and embraced the officer, encouraging him to walk outside with him and sing along. When they were out in the alley, the Underground leader took out a knife and stuck the German in the throat. As he walked back, he saw a Frenchman trying to sweet talk her into going home with him. Rodin asked the man what he wanted with his wife. The masher turned white and made a hasty exit. Liana asked La Monde to escort her home. They sang all the verses of "It's a Long Way to Tipperary" all the way to her apartment and "God Save the Queen" after which they made passionate love. In the morning, their throats were hoarse, and neither could walk, so they stayed in bed and did it again. Over time Liana began to see the double game he was playing and joined in the duplicity.

Liana caught onto the double game that Rodin was playing and joined him in it. On one occasion, he played a pro Vichy prostitute leading some German officers to a hidden allied air base, in the guise of Rebaza, while she pretended to be an Underground male that had been caught by the Gestapo and traded his life for taking the Nazis to a secret arms cache. They led them into a machine gun nest of American infantry men. The Germans were slaughtered.

The war ended and La Monde and his female companion went to Vietnam under the nationalistic guise they had worked so hard to create. It was 1946, and Ho Chi Minh had organized the Vietminh to further confuse the French, disorganized by the war. A propaganda machine was set up that fed the villages and reminded the people in them about the guillotined youth who had dared to stand up to this European invader that used their women and exploited their resources. They also denounced the Americans that boasted of their democracy, yet backed a colonial power out of fear of expanding communism. He and Liana were part of the anti West propaganda machine. The Japanese had made use of tunnels, as part of their strategy in their Asian war. Liana and Rodin used this, whether or not using this device was an invention of General Giap or a memory of the Japanese invaders. Liana and Rodin became part of training the farmers to use such weaponry against France. They were also part of the movement to not support the monarchy proposed that was within the French Union. Dressed as Rebaza, La Monde railed against the death of a son who had died in the war for France so that they could starve at the hands of this European opportunist that was no better than the Nazis were to them.

Suspicion was being aroused, and the couple had to go underground until the agents of the intruder had started to stop asking questions of the other French colonials. They began to pursue their cover jobs as a photographer for a magazine and a historian from the Sorbonne until Dien Bien Phu, where Rodin caused confusion by going back and forth through the French battleground and the Vietnamese by going back and forth through tunnels. Liana continued to lie low.

After France lost its Vietnam colonial privileges, Rodin and Liana felt that they had to mosey on down the line. Their next stop was Quebec. The Parti Quebec had been agitating for freedom from Britain. But Rodin had other ideas. From the British side, Liana sat in on Parliamentary sessions and brought up the issues of bringing Papist doctrine and Mafia influence to a free country. She also talked about the effect of losing the tourist trade, industry, and trade advantage with France, by having an alliance with part of the British Commonwealth. From the Quebekan side, Rodin talked about America and Britain being allies, and a loss of British protection possibly meaning a loss of friendly relations with America. He also stressed that this could initiate a new version of the One Hundred Years' War between France and Britain and as well as weaken the economic effects of being tied to Britain, while sacrificing friendly relations with the U.S.A. because of the common Anglo/American history. He also discussed the economic advantages of being tied to the British Commonwealth and the healthy tourist trade with the U.S.A. They lectured at universities in Toronto, Ottawa, Alberta, Manitoba, British Columbia, McGill University, University of Montreal, and Concordia University. They went to resort camps in both Ontario and Quebec to spread their propaganda and create an agitated atmosphere against further connection to France.

Rodin, in one instance gathered a group of students at the park that was made out of the battlefield at the Plains of Abraham and reminded them of the battle fought, in which French clumsiness cost them Quebec, and how France was so unstable after the war that it could not even keep a government together. He reminded them that the French and Indian War was the tail end of the One Hundred Years' War and, for all the talk of the "Glory that was France", they lost the war. He also stated that, de Gaulle to whom they were looking for leadership, was hiding in England for a good part of the war shooting his mouth off on the radio, instead of fighting. Of course, both of them gave false names and wore disguises so that they were unrecognizable. This caused the French Government to discount their importance.

They met in Toronto and went to see the museums and a Latin American festival that had very sensuous music and dances that really turned both of them on sexually. That night in their hotel room Liana came to Rodin in a low cut, backless, translucent mini gown that stressed her pointed nipples and her long, shapely legs. She felt his tumescence and took it in her hand. He groaned and started to undress and let her finish the process for him. She lay down on the bed and slowly began to wriggle out of the gown pulling the still swollen

Rodin down to her. Before entering her, he began to kiss her thighs and the triangle between them. As he entered her he began to nuzzle her thighs and her hardened nipples and her large apple shaped breasts, touching one and kissing the other. She moaned and begged him to take her. They began to rock together, and the room seemed to shake. They were as one and wanted their lovemaking to go on forever. Their juices met, and they fell exhaustedly asleep in each others' arms.

They also went to Haiti, French Guiana, and any other place where there might be any hint of French influence to be sought and undermined whatever grain of it was possible. They also repeated the process of using false names and disguises that rendered them unrecognizable. They even went back to France itself and pointed out that the growing population of Arabs was creating a minority that agitated against the past brutalities that occurred when the countries were colonies, and they brought a growing amount of hatred against Jews with them. It was translated by physical individual attacks and destruction of temples. This created pockets of dissension that were expressed in newspapers, discussions in shuls, and meetings of the legislature.

The couple felt that they were achieving a certain notoriety as dissenters, and, in order to prevent the government from launching a full blown investigation, they decided to curtail their activities and concentrate more on lovemaking. During this period Rodin began to question the decision his family held about vengeance, and he began to share his queries with Liana. She, at first, was reluctant to give up the excitement, but it was replaced with an urge for motherhood.

When Rodin met Malkia and Craine in Lafayette Escadrille, he had no idea that he would become so attached to them. He at first saw them as an instrument to learn how to smuggle information to his family, as he saw them do. His aim was to use France to understand their strategy and employ the skills he learned against them in their empire. The love he learned for them marred his clever intention to just use them to learn how to defeat his mortal enemy. This would re-enter his persona when he learned that revenge was a sickness.

Chapter 3

The couple decided to visit America. They saw the sites in New York and found what a fast, exciting town it could be. Rodin was jogging and was approached by an attractive prostitute. Immediately after he refused her wares, he was attacked by a pimp and three cohorts. To satisfy them he reached into his pocket to get a wallet and pulled out a knife and slashed the nearest one across his nose. While the thug tried to stop the bleeding, in a swift motion, the renegade Frenchman slammed his fist into another's ribs, and the bone could be heard cracking, as the would-be assailant fell to the ground. The third tried to put his hands up, but Rodin was already angered and grabbed the outstretched arm and broke it at the elbow. His parting words to the trio were, "How you make your bed is how you sleep in it. Have a nice nap, boys." In another incident, he and Liana were in front of the Yiddish library, and he wanted to show off that he understood the Jewish language from some of his experiences (which stemmed from Malkia teaching it to him) and went inside and read a Yiddish dictionary to her. When they came out, a young man, dressed as a mime walked behind Liana and pulled up her skirt. Again, Rodin found himself grabbing an arm and hearing bones crack.

They found the food exotic in New York, and the city was a lot of fun. They enjoyed baseball games and Broadway plays, but the excitement was too much like Vietnam and wartime France. They wanted a little history and culture so they went to New England. They saw the House of the Seven Gables and stopped at the Von Trapp Farm in New Hampshire and heard the beautiful music brought over from Austria by this brave family. They toured the Green Mountains, where Ethan Allen fought. Then they went south into Virginia to a historical town where a mock Revolutionary War battle was fought, and they saw a very Jewish appearing man dressed as an American Continental Soldier screaming about kicking that damn Brit's arse back to London town where he could go back to peddling stinking fish to Sherlock Holmes and Winston Churchill. A younger man, much bigger than him, and a once sturdy, older man were trying to restrain him. Rodin was curious about them. Something about the older fellow looked familiar.

Unable to stifle his curiosity, Rodin asked the older gentleman his name. His feisty response was to ask him, who in the blarney was this fart of a Frog to be asking about him. Rodin told the old gentleman that he resembled someone he once knew, but he was much older and gave him his name. All of a sudden the old codger's eyes seemed to light up. He said he was Tyndall Mikawber, and his friends were Moses and Mendel Doleman. Rodin related how he knew Craine and Malkia in Lafayette Escadrille and how he helped Patrick get out of France during the war.

All crowded around the couple and asked for war stories from both wars. They went home and got drunk on Stout and ale.

Mc Tavish called Craine, and he, Pat and his girlfriend, and Molly (whom Craine had by now married) said they would be down in a few hours, as long as it took to drive. When they got there Rodin, Craine, and Pat talked about old times and updated each other. Craine shamefacedly owned up about his activity with Dinty O'Banion, Bugs Moran, and the labor unions. Molly was not shocked about this revelation. He also told Rodin about how the Ornams had tormented his family, how they had killed Malkia, and how he had paid them back and run away from Ireland. Likewise Rodin related how and why his family had a hatred for France, and described his and Liana's activities in Algeria, the French Foreign Legion, France during and after WWII, Canada, Haiti, French Guiana, and Vietnam. Craine laughed heartily and said, "Brother, I thought I was bad. You sure weren't anybody's slouch. You have to watch the quiet ones." Pat added that it took brains to get him and Corlando out of France. He further related that Corlando had had a relationship with the factory girl he picked up when they blew the munitions plant. He ended up marrying her, and they lived somewhere around Harvard. He heard that he lucked into some stocks and had all kinds of money.

In fact he and his girl, Randi had gone to a movie and ran into him and his wife at Your Father's Mustache in Cambridge. They laughed over old time antics during the war. Randi nudged him and asked what he had to tell her about his growing up. Pat smiled and told her about trying to pick up a very beautiful German girl, who was a few years older than him in a German bar just before he came home. No one was getting anywhere with her because she was so experienced, compared to these young G.I.'s looking for a piece of tail. Since he knew Yiddish, German came easy to him, and he could communicate with her. When she wasn't looking, he took a pen and wrote a number on his arm. Seeing the number on his arm, which he obviously displayed for her, she asked if he had been in a concentration camp. He relayed to her that his parents took a trip to Poland in September 1939. He was a baby at the time. They were driving through the Carpathian Mountains, when a Stuka dive bomber shot a rocket at the car. His parents were killed, and he was thrown into the bushes and put into an orphanage. The Nazis emptied out the orphan home and sent him to Auschwitz because he was a Jew. He was young and small and could crawl through holes in the fence and carry messages to the underground. He spent the war years doing this until he was able to escape. Pat said he took the young lady home with tears in her eyes for him. He said it was the best sex he had ever had. Tyndall, Craine, his uncles, Moses and Mendel all laughed and expressed their views of his manly prowess. Randi smiled and said, "My guy is a bullshitter. The Carpathian Mountains do not go into Poland. They end in Austria." He turned red at being caught, and she stroked his face lovingly. He said he knew this, but the German girl did not, to save face. The others laughed at him.

When Rodin and Liana were back in their room, she began to communicate to him that she was available to him. He asked what caused this sudden interest. She motioned to him and whispered in his ear that she wanted his baby. He stated that he wanted this too, but the life they had chosen took risks. He asked if she wanted to risk the fact that one or both of them wanted children. She answered what was important was that a new generation emerge to right what they felt was wrong with the world. She felt that she had a good man that would love her child the way she loved him: a child raised in love would be loving and work for a loving world. With that end to their discussion, Rodin picked her up and carried her to their bed. They loved each other for several hours after that.

The next day all the troops toured Civil War sites and went spelunking in the mountains. They went down into North Carolina and saw the Cherokee Reservation that the tribe owned. They heard some talk of the Cherokees starting a business of gambling casinos in the Great Lakes area to bring money to the nation and to help other tribes that were in need. The idea sounded interesting. Another point of interest was Pat's recognizing Corlando Moran and his wife there. They renewed their acquaintance, as well as that of Rodin, who had helped get them out of France. They agreed to meet in one week at Your Father's Mustache, in Cambridge where he and Pat had last seen each other.

Chapter 4

Your Father's Mustache was a bar in the Cambridge area and was populated heavily with students from the various Boston colleges. The owners had embarked on pursuing the current trend of showing old movies. Tonight's features were *Little Caesar* with Edward G. Robinson and *Public Enemy* with Jimmy Cagney. The atmosphere was just as informal as in the old days. Customers would sample the free peanuts and throw the shells on the floor. The movies were funny to all of them, but Craine was really roaring at the imitations of the people with whom he had actually rubbed elbows. His son, Randi, and Molly ribbed him about several lines, particularly Jimmy's line about his brother, "Goin' to school to loin how to be dumb." They all had a good laugh about that. Corlando's wife, LeBere was getting on the chunky side and was teased a lot about it. Randi whispered to Molly and Liana about it; after the movies, when a karaoke was held, all three girls got on stage wearing white tee shirts they had in their handbags and started to sing a song from *South Pacific*. They rang out with, "A hundred and one tons of fun. That's my little honey bun. Look at all the fun me and Honey have." LeBere was not to be out done. She got up on stage and belted out with, "My is a crazy chick; 6 feet tall and a quarter inch thick." They all laughed and hugged, about them emphasizing a Yiddish accent, only one of which was fake. Michael and Moses.

Now it was the guys' turn. Tyndall and Moses got up and sang *Sweet Molly Malone*, both played *She'll be Comin' Round the Mountain* on a wash basin and a harmonica, while Pat yodeled it and Corlando danced to it, wearing a tutu. LeBere ran up on the stage and pinched him on his thigh. He limped off stage and screamed, "By God, she crippled me, did my Little Honey Bun."

Their mirth was cut short by three bruisers teasing a little oriental fellow, who appeared to be having the shakes. They heard: "Look at the little Gook. Couldn't win the war he picked with us at Pearl Harbor, so he comes here, lives off of us on Welfare because of a gimpy leg, then has the nerve to become a junkie. Let's teach him we don't appreciate losers and beggars." They started shoving him and slamming him against the wall. One of them reared back his fist to give him a haymaker, when Tyndall and Moses picked him up in the air and threw him in the street. He got up to face McTavish and Craine. Craine threw him back down, and McTavish stepped on his neck. The other two had to face Brython, Mendel, and Michael. They did not move a muscle. "Little Gook, is it. They used to call me Little Jew boy. Care to try that one?" piped in Moses. He added, "Get your bigoted arses out of here while we give you the chance." They picked themselves up and ran, as fast as they could. The group picked up the oriental and took him home and helped him clean up. They found out his name was Ki Lond. He was the first born in this country to Jimi Lond, who had immigrated to America when the militarists seized power in Japan. Jimi had used his last money to buy into a shoe store and wanted to prove to the Westerners that he was a loyal American. His effort was rewarded by a Nisei camp. He died there and asked his oldest son to show his loyalty to his new home. Ki joined the Marines and fought on Iwo Jima and Guadalcanal. He was horrified that he had to shoot at people that had taken refuge in caves and had no food, but they would commit Hara Kari because of the shame of surrender. He saw an officer do this to himself, but he was not allowed to register any sympathy for him to his American buddies because they'd see him as a traitor. That would be breaking his promise to his father. He was haunted by the picture of the officer's suicide that kept coming up in his dreams.

After the war, he wandered around Asia plagued by the recurrent vision and found that opium could provide relief. He wandered from Iwo Jima and Guadalcanal to Okinawa to Japan to China to Burma to India to Afghanistan with the faces of the officer gutting himself plaguing his vision day and night for two years after the war and his father's image extracting a promise from him he could not keep. He also saw the pleading eyes of the Japanese soldiers emerging from the caves, as he shot them. Ki stowed away on a ship, heading for San Francisco. He wandered around the states smoking and shooting up drugs to blot out his pain until he reached the point of only wanting the drug and forgetting what he wanted to relieve. From city to city and state to state he became an object of ridicule and abuse until that night in Cambridge. Craine and Rodin got him into a rehabilitation program, had constant contact with his counselors and doctors, and closely monitored his progress for a year until they were sure he was clean. Then Corlando hired him as a chauffeur, handyman, and gardener. This later proved to be a wise investment in a human being.

In the meantime Rodin and Liana decided to settle down in the Pittsburgh area so that they could be between their friends and not too far away. Liana's drive for motherhood continued to drive Rodin crazy, but he found that it was a pleasant route to insanity. They really could not get enough of each other. They became the proud parents of twins: a boy and a girl. Craine offered Rodin a partnership in his trucking firm because Pat was not interested and was pursuing a career with an eye to starting his own airline.

All seemed to be going well for the two old friends, whose relationship spanned two wars and a cold one, followed by a hot one, but one of the hooligans that had jumped Ki saw something familiar about McTavish Mikawber. Tandry Obrits, the bully that had a foot placed on his neck, had a memory of being strongly anti union way back in the days when he worked in a factory in Belfast. He had an argument with McTavish and gotten a shiner for it, a shiner he never forgot. A few years later, a story went around Belfast that a family, with whom the Mikawbers had differences was wiped out by a mysterious strafing by an airplane. After he stowed away on a boat to Boston he had heard rumors of a companionship between someone named Craine and Dinty O'Banion, Bugs Moran, and an episode of violent pro union agitation that had cost his friend, Albert Grayson, his factory, and being destitute had caused him to later jump out a fifteen story window. Perhaps, the threat of a few words in the right places could be profitable to Tandry.

However, he'd have to investigate the facts first. He would see if the IRA and any remaining Ornams wanted the information.

McTavish paid the bully no mind, but he wondered why he was looking at him so strangely, as if there was some connection between them. He told Craine about it, who couldn't fathom why he had looked at his brother in such a bizarre way. Craine had never seen Tandry. However, Tyndall remembered something about a black eye, and it all came back to McTavish. He went after Tandry and tackled him. He was placed in a barrel of cucumbers that were about to be mixed with brine and dills and sent to a training center for St. Bernards in the French Alps, as a treat for the dedicated staff.

Chapter 5

Corlando and LeBere were unable to have children, and this was always an unhappy spot in their life together, particularly around holiday times. They would get out their trailer at these times and travel to lands unknown to lessen the painful preoccupation with cookouts, gift giving occasions, birthday celebrations that took up families' times. This year they decided to travel to the Western half of the country: the Dakotas, Wisconsin, Montana, Washington, Wyoming, Colorado, New Mexico, Texas, Oklahoma, Nebraska, Louisiana, the Carolinas, and home to the East Coast around Christmastime.

Fargo, North Dakota was an icy, isolated section of the country. Because most Americans preferred more catering to tourists, places where food could be grown, or wild nightlife or cultural outlets, the Dakotas were not overly populated.

Corlando and LeBere were bored with the isolation and cold. They wanted to hear children laughing, hubbubs while shopping, and hear people exchanging greetings and laughing, even they would be only outside participants. They were set to go home, they could be where they would be lonely without traveling hundreds of miles. All of a sudden, they heard a startling noise. A wiry boy, fourteen or fifteen years old, with a small boy with him was holding off a gang of angry teenagers. They had ball bats and chains, and were calling him a thief. The boy snatched one bat out of one kid's arms and started to swing it.

Corlando went back to his car and held a shotgun in one hand and a tire iron in the other. He addressed the gang thusly: "This is a democracy; you have a choice of whether you want to face Elmer or the tire iron." They all lowered their tools of destruction and sat in the direction he motioned with Elmer. He then said, "About thirty years ago I fought in a war that was fought, in part, so that kids your age would benefit from fair laws that said things like, 'Innocent until proven guilty.' Anybody got any proof." A tall red haired boy piped up with: "This Redskin just stole a Game Boy out of Kids R Us. We don't hold with thievin' Redskins." Corlando looked at the Indian boy and said: "You know that war I told you about; we fought on an island in the Pacific overrun with Japanese, and we needed the land for airstrips to end the war. One of the men that raised our flag that protects the freedom about which I told you was an Indian. I don't think he'd take kindly to the word 'Redskin'. Let's see what his story is.

The Native American let a tear fall that was a mixture of anger, sadness, and frustration at not being allowed to fight back. Then he let loose with his story. "I'm a Blackfoot. The Indian agent at the Reservation had a gambling problem and stole our food stamps to sell them to get sharks off of him to pay back a debt. Our parents went to Washington D.C. to complain to our congressman with 50 others. They were met by Klansmen. My father was killed by a brick to the head, and my mother was raped and killed so she couldn't tell anyone. I don't want any nosy, crooked-assed social worker stepping into our life and separating us. I heard a white boy at school telling a friend he wanted a Game Boy for Christmas, and his father just got laid off of his job. It's me that has to feed Bobby and me. I don't need any handouts from OFAYS that only know to call me Redskin. I took it to sell it to him." The other boys put down their bats and chains and reached into their wallets. The boy said, "I appreciate your kindness, but I meant what I said about handouts. They say to me that you're better than me because you can give to a miserable slob that can't take care of himself. What was taken from me, I can take back. Don't preach to me about the Loving God and send me to a useless school. Give me a job so I can do what a man is supposed to do: take care of his family." He took his brother's hand and walked away.

The conversation was not whispered and not screamed, but there was emotion felt and emotion expressed. LeBere had heard every word. She could not hide the tears that had dried on her face, and Corlando had a hard time choking them back, himself. They tried to drown out the sadness and admiration for the chutzpah in the face of hopelessness and prejudice. They remembered the writings of an Afro-

American writer, James Baldwin, who spoke about people respecting people that they had to deal with as brokers, and did not respect those to whom they gave out of Noblesse Oblige. They asked themselves how could this tough little man child have his fight transformed so that he could be a broker, not a beggar. They did not go home, but stayed in Fargo to address this issue that nagged at them.

Through discreet questioning of the local congressman, they learned that the lad was named Donny Clippingbird. He was very bright in school but organized his abilities in a pattern similar to the Pan Indian movement of Tecumseh. Only their aim was not creating a cultural entity to stand up to the white man but to train for mutual self defense against him. Self defense that sent bullies home limping and bleeding. Corlando saw to it that a karate school opened up near the reservation with an instructor, who was a Native American, looking for recruits and an assistant. Of course, Donny did not know who was behind the school.

The couple went back to Boston to face the good cheer of a Christmas without children. They spent a lot of time talking about how brave and good Donny was in raising Bobby alone. He was not exactly like a mother bear protecting her cub, more like a lion king protecting its pride. He seemed to be almost intuitive in absorbing the philosophy of James Baldwin without ever having been exposed to its contents. They wrote to their contact with the congressman from North Dakota to set up a contest, whereby the winner would get a trip to Washington D.C. and assume the role of the congressman from the district for a week and stay at the home of a chosen sponsor. They had planned to rig it so that Donny won, but he was bright enough to do it on his own merits. That they would be selected to be the sponsor could easily be faked to look like coincidence. Corlando teased LeBere about arranging their meeting at the munitions plant and making it look like a similar coincidence. She laughed and said, "Sure, you deliberately chose a plant where I worked, didn't you." He said that's not where the planning came in. "It happened when I first saw you." She laughed again and said: "Yeah, bending over, showing you and the world what I had to offer." "Oh yes, but it was me that saw the jewelry in that bent position, and I think we both profited from it, my dear. In fact, let's go

upstairs and reap the benefits of my nosy introduction to the fair sex."
That's just what they did.

The next week, the contest winner and his baby brother were
surprised to be welcomed to the home of the Morans. Corlando went
to congress with Donny and listened to the teenager debate
representatives, as well as senators to a standstill. They all knew that
this youth would get somewhere with or without the help of wealth.
There was more culture to which this young fighter could be exposed,
and he seemed to be destined to not only fight, but lead. However, the
direction of this leadership could be colored by a violent, hostile
beginning or application of principles that could raise him out of the
mire of an angry beginning.

The couple began to take the two boys to The Smithsonian
Institute, The Museum of Science and Industry, the Federal Mint,
Arlington Cemetery, where they saw the graves of Joe Louis, Lee
Marvin, and Ira Hayes. They enjoyed the drama of *The Glass
Menagerie*, by Tennessee Williams and discussed the changes
Corlando encountered in the war. Donny enjoyed the fight of a
Brooklyn Doctor for decency for his patients in *The Last Angry Man*
and the compassion a young hardened businessman learned for his
newly introduced brother in the movie *Rain Man*. At the end of the
week Donny hugged Corlando and LeBere and said, "I wish you were
our parents." And so they were.

The process was not that simple. The Morans and the two boys had
to return to Fargo and face the Reservation, The Indian agent, The
Adoption Board and several other worthless bureaucrats that smiled a
lot and used fifty dollar words, where a twenty-five cent one would
have sufficed. Donny laughed inside and thought about Ira Hayes, who
was driven to an alcoholic death by drowning because fools like these
had turned the simple patriotic act of raising the flag on Mt. Suribachi
into a fiasco to sell war bonds and entangled the heroes into such a
mess that Americanism, patriotism, or any natural emotion was
supplanted by the expedience of idiocy to the extent of having no
worthwhile meaning. God, politicians and bureaucrats added their own
stink to life. After an interminable tolerance of this garbage, Bobby
and Donny Clippingbird had a new family. They went to say goodbye

to their best friends, the Hardydove family. Becky Hardydove was only thirteen, compared to Donny's age of fifteen and a half. But she was already having to fight off the advances of the gambling, crooked Indian agent and a couple congressmen. A tear trickled down her face, as Donny took her hand and Bobby hugged her, as if she were the mother he had lost two years ago. They vowed to meet again in two years and take up their lives again. The howl of a lone coyote brought the heartbreak of their separation to a head, and Donny remembered the way he protected her from the fear of the single howl when he was eight and a half and she was six. She drew herself to the angle between his arm and chest and said: "May the wind that bears you away to your destiny bring you back to me as my Man." He and Bobby walked back to the Lodge where LeBere and Corlando were waiting for the boys. Donny looked back, but he never went back to the reservation. However, he did remember the Blackfoot Tribe, and they had sufficient cause to remember him.

Section III

Donny Clippingbird

Chapter 1

Donny and Bobby became the Moran boys. They dearly loved their new parents. The karate school secretly begun by Corlando was an integral part of their education. Both boys had achieved black belt status by the time they were eighteen. Donny had made his bones by the time of majority and so did Bobby. They also did not forget their origins. There was frequent communication with Becky Hardydove. In fact, she was a frequent visitor to their home. There was also frequent communication with the Mikawber/Dolemans and the La Mondes. Bobby's and Donny's substitute for a big brother was Ki Lond. He introduced them to sifting out worthwhile friends from shiftless bums, spotting a hot chick in a crowd and separating her from verbalizing, scared girls, never to give an enemy strength over themselves with big mouthed information or gestures of bravado or to give a female any strength over them by the victimization that gossip brought. The condom was introduced to both brothers, as a means of preserving freedom; he taught both Donny and Bobby to use their karate skills with responsibility and the difference from picking fights and resisting being picked on. He told them about wearing the condom while enjoying the fruits of sex. He taught them the rudiments of pool and billiards, to the point of having an easy way to earn lunch money. He showed the boys how to discipline themselves from the costs of stealing, drug, sexual, gambling, power and money addictions, as well as how to spot these traits in others. He also taught the striplings to avoid the revels of being led by angry, sympathetic, overly callous responses to the imprecations of have nots.

Now Donny was of high school age. He had already confided his views of the corruption and fallibility of the white man, but he was also encouraged by Ki and others to see white men, such as Craine,

Rodin, Moses, Tyndall as humans with plenty of good along with the bad. He also could not help but seeing the good and compassionate along with the evil by which they and others judged and feared them. The oaths and curses were secondary to the love they felt for each other and humanity. Donny chose to listen to his father and attend Phillip Exeter Academy because he wanted to develop the skills to recreate the Pan Indian Movement of Tecumseh. He started out by winning respect from a Preppy, who called him Tonto every time he saw him. The lad was a football player and outweighed Donny by 30 lbs and stood a head taller than him. All of a sudden he found himself in a wrist lock that threatened to break his hand off if he didn't kneel down and recite "O wa tagu Siam." Donny also worked for his meals in a girls' dorm. Several of the young ladies were interested in his dark good looks. Even though he would engage in flirtations, his heart belonged to Becky. She was a frequent visitor to his home, and he visited her at the reservation.

Donny had proven his mastery of the physical prowess in the dorm, but he also recognized that he had to dispel the anger that carried him through the years in Fargo. He became a wrestler and was called 'Tonto the Gladiator', which was shortened to Gladiator. His knowledge was brought to the fore when he showed the boys in his dorm how to fend off Alkies and Druggies by setting up the thug who attacked a single boy returning home from study at the library or a date and lifting the fat wallet he carried. The single boy would be bait for a gang of students waiting with baseball bats to beat the hell out of the thug. Word got around, and the entrepreneurial tribesman was teaching martial arts to male and female alike.

The second part of his rebuild Tecumseh program was to excel academically. He would spend four hours a night in the library, review his class notes from the beginning once a week, and keep up with his reading assignments. He would also participate in class discussions and ask questions about what he didn't understand. No one realized what his real goal was except Becky and his brother. Sometimes they were frightened of the seemingly unceasing fire that drove him, but it drove him nonetheless. When they questioned him about it, his answer was, "We deserve a piece of this country too. We died in its wars along with Afro-Americans, Hispanics, Jews, Italians, Germans, Poles, and Russians. White does not necessarily make it right." Becky would take his arm, give him a little girl's pout, snuggle close to him, and say that they had to accept the world the way it is. He'd try not to laugh and would tell her all she was accomplishing was to make him erect. Now, if they went anywhere, she'd have to walk in front of him. She laughed and kissed him quickly before she got in front, hanging onto his hand. He laughed and let himself be led

Donny didn't have much money to waste, but he noticed the preppies in his dorm did. They were always looking for ways to get thrills and would throw money around. They frequented bars and joked about getting as drunk as a Sioux Indian or as sotted as Sitting Bull. They ran to strip bars and couldn't wait to unload their fat bankrolls for a lap dance. There were frequent crap games or stud poker games in the dorms. As much as $500.00 was dropped in a game. Needless to say, the young Blackfoot put this behavior in context with the remarks about the drunkenness and set several of the spoiled white brats up in spending their easily gotten money on the stupidity they wanted to do and charged them a commission for showing them their pleasure sites. He even split the fees of a prostitute with her for bringing several of the suckers to her.

The thrill of getting something for nothing always played an important role in the preppies lives. For this reason, Donny set up gambling games with townies in back alleys and told the greedy, lazy kids he knew where and when they were. He got a commission from the bookies that organized the fetes. He even set up poker games in hotels with known gangsters and watched the fools lose their fat money from their parents to some of the same men, who used to roll them. This was not without creating suspicions from Corlando, who wondered why his son always had money to spend but never had to ask him for it. Having gone this route in the service, he knew that he would not learn anything by asking his son. Therefore, he decided to learn by watching and tailing Donny to the gambling/prostitution sites.

Corlando had experienced a tough youth, which drove him to enlist in the service, more by cops being after him and judges being an inch from offering him reformatories for his activities. He knew plenty of pimps, bookies, and numbers runners. He made a few contacts and told them to burst his son's bubble, but not to hurt him too bad, just bad enough to scare him.

That Saturday, Donny set fifteen guys up with a call girl and two friends for a series of threesomes. The madam for whom they worked was an old flame of his father's, who was acquainted through work with many rough looking and acting pimps. After the threesomes, Donny was pretty happy about the tight little wad of money he had made. He was surprised when three huge men approached him as he took a shortcut across an alley to get to the dorm. One had a blackjack, one had brass knuckles, and one had a German Luger he had brought back from the war. The nearest one said in a quiet voice that appeared to be suppressing a great deal of anger, "Hey, man, we've been noticing our ladies have been short on the green they've been turning in to us. We're also into suckering some of these gambling junkies into parting with their money for our benefit; there have been shortages there .There's not a new kid on the block is there? We think there is, and we just found him." Donny began to stammer about this being a country of free enterprise, and surely they didn't object to spreading the money around. The second man chuckled and said, "I mind spreading mine around; I call that stealing."

He started to swing at Donny's jaw with the brass knuckles. But the lad blocked the blow and delivered a karate kick to the man's scrotum, which the hooligan sidestepped and delivered his metallic smack. He drew blood. One of the others moved behind the youthful warrior and lashed across his ear with the blackjack. Donny whirled around and went for his throat, but the man caught his hand and delivered another blackjack blow to his hand. The third abandoned his Luger, reached for his knife, and cut Donny's belt off his pants so that they fell to the ground. The men picked his pants up, emptied the money out of his wallet, and threw it back to him. They took his pants and warned him that next time he tried to play man they'd take his ass, and all the fancy Karate wouldn't do a damn thing to stop it. The man with the blackjack put his instrument aside and cuffed the lad on the back of his head. To drive the lesson further home, Donny's Human Behavior teacher (who had been approached by Corlando) gave an assignment to do extensive research on how playing on people's perversions for gain ended in several negative consequences and to derive and prove a theory that applied to this that had irrevocable postulations, as well as rigorous theorems backing them up that provided undisputable proof to back up the hypothesis that was stated by the assignment. Each student had to present this to the class in one week. The sores plus the stiff academic exercise proved to be quite instructive to the bright, scheming student.

Donny was off from school for Thanksgiving weekend, when his father told him how he found out about his enterprises. He also told the boy how he had schemed to teach him a lesson he would not forget so quickly, and he related some of his pre-war and wartime experiences that helped teach him the concepts he had attempted to implant to his son. He told him about how Rodin La Monde had rescued him and his uncle Pat. How he had to shoot kids at Remagen to get across the German/French border. He reminded him that these kids would never get the opportunity to have the choice presented to them that he had. They were dead, as he might very well have been. He talked about General Patton's men and the Tuskegee Airmen who were Afro-American and who had served their country and bled from Africa up the boot of Italy into France only to return to ungrateful prejudice and racism. He pointed out that they also had to choose to either live decent lives or sacrifice them fighting the losing battle in which Donny had engaged. He also urged his son to talk to Ki, who could tell him of the choices that had to be made in the Pacific War, and what he had to face to make these choices.

Donny heard his father, but it was years later that he had to act on the thoughts his Dad had tried to implant in him. The bitterness he carried against the white race was complicated by two factors: The pain was deep and cruel; The anger was earned. Yet he loved his parents, and this might yet sustain his human feelings. Despite the harshness of these lessons, a deep bitterness had been implanted in Donny, and it would take the combined love of his mother and father, Bobby and Becky, to dispel it. To this would be added the experiences of Craine, Rodin, the rest of the Mikawbers, and the inevitable consequences of living a life of hate and desire for revenge.

So many of us carry the pollution of suspicion, mistrust, and failure to understand one another, and shut out communication with each other because of the fear erected by dealing with someone different. We can share our intelligences with one another to fight global warming or hunger instead of labeling ourselves as good and evil and trying to wipe each other out.

Chapter 2

Ki was busy washing the car when he saw his young friend, Donny approaching. He had heard about his antics and his father's unique answer to it. He also heard the Dad/son conversation through the open windows since LeBere was a fresh air fiend. "What's up, Chief," the chauffeur asked. Donny gave his mentor and friend a knowing look. "I'm sure you know the mess I've recently brought on myself, and I am also sure you heard the dialogue between me and my father just now." Ki indicated that Donny's perceptions were accurate. He told him that, as his father was dying he made a promise to him to redeem the honor of his family in the eyes of the Americans because he had chosen to leave the imposed tyranny that had overtaken his land in the name of the code of the warrior, Bushido. He had perceived this part of a repetition of Hitler's tactics of using emotional appeals to persuade a suffering people to summon forth the suppressed ego structures of their culture and make them blind to fairness and justice. Ki swore to his father that he would do this. A Physical Education teacher had chosen Ki as his example of the awkward teenager to pick on in front of the other teens looking for identities. The word, Jap or Nip, was always used as an epithet that meant more marching after class or swats for bad behavior that were either non-existent or provoked. His response was to struggle through a school where he was hated due to politics and propaganda. He did manage to graduate. He performed two tasks before leaving L.A. He encountered his nemesis, the teacher, who made a snide remark. On a reflex action, he slugged him in the jaw and watched his false teeth fall to the ground. He ground them to bits with his foot and left the coach to deal with what the other students had to say. The year was 1941, and a Japanese, showing up at the draft board to enlist brought forth suspicion and surprise. This was step one in his promise to his father and to the nation his family had chosen to make their home, choosing a chance for justice over wanton tyranny and self destruction. He didn't know if he was gambling in vain against the hatred that seemed to dominate the world. He joined the marines on the same day he had rendered a bully, as toothless.

He found a hodgepodge of young men in boot camp; some joined up with the law at their heels, some were brimming with patriotism and high ideals, some had nowhere else to go. He met two young men that would affect his values for the rest of his life. One was a Pima Indian from Arizona, whose family were starving farmers on their reservation. The other was a Chicano from East L.A., who was adopted at age 12 by a Japanese family, which was interned at a Nisei concentration camp. Their names were Ira Hayes and Guy Gabaldon. These two young men inspired Ki to the point of enduring the senseless, cruel taunts that drove him many times to strike back. Finding these soldiers to be the exception, rather than the rule after the war later caused him to wander the world and to embrace the quagmire of the world, called drugs. However, he was able to find his way back to their ideals through the help of others, such as Donny's father.

The weekend we finished boot camp, our squad went out to get drunk. We saw four Germans cornering a Jewish kid and blaming him for getting us into the war. The one nearest me was mad because he had to leave his girl behind, and she was the best lay in his high school district. They pushed him against the wall, and he fell. They got on top of him and started to slug his face. One of them smashed a beer bottle, the way it was in *From Here to Eternity*, and held it to his eyes. Guy raced up there and pulled the guy away from him and threw him up against the wall with such force that the beer bottle flew from his hand. The rest of us moved up to keep others from joining in the fight. One of the Germans noticed me and said, "Looky, looky we have one of the famous guests that brought us the now well known Pearl Harbor show." They all looked toward me and started to move. Guy threw a chair in front of them and said, "What is this war about? Do you believe we can fight against racism and go on being racists? If we aren't going to give that up, we might as well not be fighting because we're no different than the Nazis and militarists that pushed us into the war." There was a silent moment as one of the Germans helped the Jewish kid to his feet. They turned away from me, but no one said he was sorry. I was used to that, but, at least, Guy kept them off of me. He hugged me, and we went our separate ways.

I was being sent to the Pacific Theater of Operations. At Midway, we slowed the Japanese advance down, but the Japs were building an airstrip in the Solomons on Guadalcanal that could allow the enemy to advance on Australia. With MacArthur crawling up the back of New Guinea, air support was needed to help him and to be a guard against Japanese advance on Australia, an important ally. We landed on Guadalcanal in August of '42. The Japs had been bombing our sea support the night before. We thought we'd have an easy ride when we landed 12,000 men. I had made friends with the Jewish kid Guy had saved, as did the Germans, who had jumped him. All six of us fought our way to the airstrip. I saw one of my German buddies get it in his right eye and blood was gushing out of the right side of his head. I called for a medic, and one crawled through the mass of men. The Jewish kid was shoving men out of the way so the medic could get to him; a grenade was thrown, and all three were blown to kingdom come. I saw the eye on the ground next to the Jewish kid's body. There were just not enough Leathernecks to cover the island. We had help from the army and the Army Air Force. We fought six months on that island and lost 1,500 men and the Japanese lost 25,000, not counting those who died at sea.

We had some leave time coming. One of the Germans who were left went with me to Oahu, Hawaii. I met a beautiful girl, whose mother was from Sumatra, and whose father was Dutch. She had green, emerald eyes and a smooth, tawny skin. She was long legged and full breasted, along with having jet black hair that grew down her back. Over the span of two weeks leave, I saw her four times. We made love in the forest behind the house where she and her parents lived, the second time I saw her. On our last time together, we were attacked by a Japanese national, vacationing on Oahu. He knifed me in the diaphragm, and I lost consciousness. She was kidnapped and raped, then left for dead, which happened in the hospital. The perp belonged to a nationalist, fanatical group and was ordered to commit

Hara Kari for leaving the organization vulnerable to unfavorable publicity. I thought about her a lot on several of my island adventures. I had enough of a jolt to put my grief in perspective on Tinian and Saipan. We were starting to give Hirohito a run for his money. The allies wanted a base close to Japan to be able to send B-29's to the Japanese mainland. On June 13, 1944 the U.S. began bombing Saipan and landed on June 15. There were mountains on the island and General Saito hid his men in caves and led attacks at night. At this point, the United States used a new weapon, Guy Gabaldon. He knew street Japanese and was able to talk 1,800 Japanese into surrendering, telling the troops that Americans were not barbarians and that they could expect fair treatment. I did not have contact with him, but I was proud I knew him and remembered his courageous stand on my behalf. I also grew sad when I thought of the Jewish and German friends I had lost.

Donny asked about the Pima Indian Ki had mentioned, Ira Hayes. Ki took up the discussion with a little prelude. The Jerries seemed to know that they would lose the war after such battles as Remagen in which they had to use kids. The Japs were losing one island stronghold after another. The old guard was stubborn about losing their way of life, Bushido, the way of the warrior, and vowed to fight to the last man. The Americans, on the other hand, at least after the death of President Roosevelt, saw the end of the war in sight and put pressure on President Truman to bring the boys home. Hence they were looking for an attack point close to Japan and also a place where wounded bombers could be repaired and sent back to the fight with a minimal risk to the lives of the crews, due to ability to get to a hospital quickly. The island was Iwo Jima. It was 600 miles from the islands of Japan. The date for attack was selected as 02-19-45. In December 1944 bombing began. 80,000 marines were available. The Japanese used the strategy of hiding in caves, so that they were invulnerable to the bombings, due to this protection and could attack at night, as they did in other areas. As the men landed, they were fired upon from Mount Suribachi. This advantage had to be neutralized. For the first three days, the battle to the summit was hand-to-hand and face-to-face. We found the enemy dug in, about 2,000 of them. About 1,000 Japanese were killed on the way to the summit. About 4,500 Americans were killed on that day. Finally the peak was taken. Six of these gyrenes raised the American flag on the top. One of them was Ira Hayes. He did it because he was an American. He genuinely thought that the real heroes were the buddies that died, that wouldn't come back. He was very much surprised to be called a hero and chagrined that he was called away from the front to parade around like a hero while others continued to die, not for their country, but for a bureaucracy that used heroes to speak for them, instead of speaking for themselves about the goals of the war. The battle lasted almost a month. During this time, the Japanese lost over 21,000, and we lost 7,000. General Kurabashi committed Hara Kari. I witnessed an officer doing this, and I picked up a drug habit from the memory from the sight of it. Ira Hayes was so bothered by the hypocrisy of what he had to do that he became an alcoholic. He died frozen to death in an irrigation ditch after a drinking binge. He despaired for his people with no water, no crops, and no hope for them. He did not consider himself a hero, just thought about the buddies he had lost.

Donny asked what connection he had to Ki. The oriental looked sad and said that Ira had also protected him from mob rule. A gang had been drinking illegally in their tents and decided, as so many others had, that Ki was responsible for Pearl Harbor. Ira got in front of them with a shovel and told the mob they had to get through him first. They backed down. At this point, a tear came to the eye of the chauffeur. He told Donny that even though he had encountered extreme prejudice, he had also encountered people that rose above this evil and that fighting at this end of the spectrum brought as much hope for mankind as standing up for the nationality inspired by the act of standing and fighting back. The fight involved the stand up pride of Malcolm X and also the love for mankind of Martin Luther King, Jr. Donny's father also adhered to this duality of wisdom by letting Donny have the opportunities to learn and observe both ends of the spectrum. At one end was Tecumseh and at the other was Sequoia, a Cherokee that translated the Bible into his native language. Donny would struggle with this concept into his adult years.

Ki also related the circumstances under which he had come to know Donny's father Craine Mikawber, Moses Doleman, and the rest of the Mikawbers. He also smiled and said, "None of us were angels either." This statement and learning these concepts later had profound effects on what Donny did with his life. As with many of us, anger and desires for vengeance intermingle with compassion and wanting to better the position of oneself with his/her view of his fellow man.

Chapter 3

There is something about the Christmas season that draws humans in predominantly Christian countries to fellowship, love, and sex as an addition to the love component. Maybe it's the latter, covered up by the artifice of love. But, at any rate, it runs rampant through our society. Donny, who fancied himself as a red-blooded young man was into the general schema. He avoided the schemes of his previous days because of the severity of the physical component to his lesson and the thought processes stimulated by his professor, his father, and Ki. He began to say yes to the young ladies, who were forever approaching him, in spite of his promise to Becky. A girl in the dorm where he worked began to tease him during working hours about his manliness and kept asking him to take her to movies, plays, school dames. She also tried to find out about his personal life, which he had learned to keep to himself. She had used inductive reasoning from his responses in class and his partiality to Amer-Indians, as testified to by his early revelation in wrestling, as well as the gossipy mouths of his dorm fellows. She concluded that he had some Amer-Indian connections and had seen much of the rough end of it.

A bunch of guys were getting together to celebrate the anniversary of the closing of the draft board back in the Nixon years. They started out by singing an old John Denver song, *The Draft Dodger Song*. They noticed some imperfection in their singing; one base held his head down and turned his collar up. Two fellows parted the open collar and saw an attractive girl wearing a fake mustache with a fake scar on her jaw line. They saw a squirrel they knew was tame and made some hand motions that indicated they had some nuts for it, then put the mustache on it and let it go. They put the scar inside of the cup of a man begging because he had halitosis and couldn't get a job.

They found out her name was Penny Pitressin, and she had a crush on Donny. "Donny? Who is Donny?" asked several voices. Penny pointed him out. "Oh. you mean the Gladiator. You don't want a roughneck like him; you want a gentleman like me," said the young man that had opened her collar. "I like to make love, not war." As he put his arm around her waist, he heard a snap and seemed to rise in the air. The snap was the fracture of his elbow joint, and the rise in the air was Gladiator pulling him off of her. A sharp voice behind him said, "She's not a piece of meat, and she doesn't need your slick pick up tactics." While the disconcerted youth went to the infirmary to have his elbow tended to, Penny slipped her arm through Donny's and asked him to walk her home.

He told her about Becky, and he said he would be faithful to her. She began to coax him to be freer with himself and not bind himself up with a commitment that would go sour in a few years, but if he counted his "Pennies," they might turn into "dollars." She moved a little closer to him and gripped his arm a little tighter. She pulled him closer to her and sought his lips. He tried to resist, but found the pressure of her tongue inside his mouth and moving against his teeth to brush his lips and her breasts pressing against his chest while her fingers pulled at his shirt impossible to do so. She kept pulling at him. When they reached a woodsy area, she pulled him behind a clump of bushes and reached for his swollen organ. She reached inside his pants and stroked him. Then she undid his zipper and took him in her mouth. After this, she began to stroke his thighs and pulled him down to her. She slid out of her trousers and thong and pulled him into her. As they began to move together, she unfastened her brassiere and slipped out of it, unbuttoned her blouse, while pressing his head against her hardening nipples. He began to kiss them and to touch her there and on her thighs, caressing her mound as he approached it. She began to moan, "Again, again I never felt so much in my life. You're beautiful." They went for two hours like this. They fell asleep after two hours and were awakened by a security guard in the morning. Both principals were contacted, and both parents were contacted for a meeting to be held the Friday before Christmas break.

Becky found out about the incident, and she also knew that Donny was facing expulsion from Phillip Exeter Academy. She would not believe Donny that Penny had seduced him and was not certain that the other boy and Gladiator hadn't set this up beforehand. She asked around the dorm and found the boy, whose elbow Donny had broken. He refused to step forward for Donny because he had lost a position on the tennis team due to his elbow and he didn't see any reason to help a no account Redskin, that was too uppity, anyway. His name was Mictal Ornam. He had had Green ancestry in Ireland who were wiped out in the rebellion. His grandfather was smart enough to leave the country and had established himself as a furrier. He had made all sorts of money, and his father was active in Tammany Hall politics.

Corlando and LeBere arrived and were crushed by the news. Penny's parents had taken her to a gynecologist. Fortunately she was not pregnant. Her mother, who had divorced her father because she hated men and had married for position, only to find he was a philanderer and a drunk, who beat her, knew of Corlando's wealth. She was dead set on separating him from it and ordered Penny to tell the school authorities that Donny had raped her.

When Corlando heard this, he was on the phone with his lawyer, Bruno Havelich. At a meeting, held fifteen minutes later Donny was explaining what had occurred to Corlando, LeBere, Becky, and Bobby. Becky had a hard time believing Donny because she knew how attractive he was to a woman and how he had related to women. Bruno asked her to stifle her doubt because a lot of character references were needed in this case, and any doubts cast in belief would be pushed to the jury by the opposition. Donny was given a lie detector test before the state could demand one. Mictal Ornam and Penny were to be questioned thoroughly by Bruno and his staff. Becky and Bobby were to be on the lookout for evidence of duplicitous character and/or promiscuity as brought out by talking to friends and enemies alike. Wires were to be worn while these talks were taking place, even though they were inadmissible in court. Bruno asked Donny and Becky to talk and iron out their areas of doubt that night, or Becky could not be part of the defense. A final part of the strategy was to file a substantial lawsuit for character assassination and hindering further potential professional development and/or pursuit.

That night Becky and Donny discussed every aspect of the activity. Donny maintained that he had told Penny that he was committed and that she could not see beyond her attraction to him or the moment in time. He wondered if Mictal and her set this up. He did note that Penny got excited very rapidly and behaved as if she had planned to be that way. She moved into the frightened maiden role rather quickly, as well as becoming affectionate very suddenly. Donny did not make the excuse that she pushed him beyond what his manhood could control. He felt some guilt in this area, and Becky recalled several instances when he wanted to go further than she would let him, and he had respected her boundaries. He said he did so because he loved her and didn't like the fact that a part of him pressured her. He also reminded Becky that Penny had pressured him, and not vice versa. Becky had to acknowledge this. Her doubt was satisfied. The physical examination of both parties, which Bruno had insisted upon, further verified removal of doubt on Becky's part. There was no scarring of vaginal tissue or signs of violence, but Donny's penis showed marks that more than suggested rough handling. Donny's lie detector test came back negative.

In the meantime, Bobby was doing some homework. He found that Mictal knew of the relationship between Corlando and the Mikawbers and about the wiping out of the Ornams in Ireland via the drunken ravings of his Uncle Tandry before his pickle of a trip to Switzerland. He also was aware of who Donny was, even though he had played dumb. He engaged Mictal in a conversation by playing one of Donny's suckers, who felt cheated by one of the prostitutes with whom he was set up. Mictal did not know Bobby from Adam and revealed what he knew into the tape recorder.

Bruno then capped the value of the data off by filing a $562,000 lawsuit for defamation of character, to be followed by a further suit that said Donny's choice of career would be limited and that his education would be affected by merely having to deal with the ugliness brought into the minds of a school, conscious of its reputation. This value was in the process of being estimated, and a figure would be arrived at shortly.

In his meanderings on campus, Donny encountered Penny, who

looked at him longingly and sadly. He was on a study break, and she approached him, saying, "I did not want to do this, but my mother hates men because her marriage went sour, due to marrying a drunken bum with erroneous plans that turned it into a horror." Donny encouraged her to tell him more by feigning sympathy and got the whole thing on his tape recorder.

Bruno thought that it was about time for the lawyers and opponents to meet. He wanted the Plaintiffs to be off guard so he arranged a luncheon to make it look as if Donny was pleading for leniency on their part. He reserved a comfortable table at Applebees for the luncheon. Bruno could see Penny's side, including the lawyer gloating inside. They had a pleasant lunch with hors d'oeuvres. The attorney was chuckling with Penny's mother and engaging in flirtatious glances. Donny had a corned beef sandwich, garnished with mustard and dill pickle and an order of home fries, followed by German chocolate cake with strawberry ice cream over it. He tried to look meek to fall in with Bruno's plan. They took a little break and were to reassemble in a room reserved by the restaurateur. They had also requested that the judge be present so that he would hear the evidence that could not be presented in court, so that he could make a decision whether to pursue the case further.

Bruno asked the Plaintiff to present its evidence and demands first. The mother nudged her attorney friend playfully, who assumed a serious pose and talked about the foulness of a deed that would force shame on an innocent, young lady and cause her to abandon her career plans, due to the embarrassment He estimated that about $500,000 would be sufficient to pay for the assault on the maiden's name. Bruno then read off the testimonies of several of Penny's friends, both male and female, who blatantly stated that Penny was no maiden. In fact, several males had made statements that they either had sex with Penny or witnessed others doing so. The dialogue with Mictal was presented, which established grounds for bias against Donny and opened up the possibility for discussion of a contrived plan between Penny and Mictal and shed a reasonable doubt upon the claim of rape. Penny's lawyer began to shift from his flirtatious and confident position to one of concern that he might lose this case; he began to show the slightest amount of perspiration on his forehead and had to take his glasses off. He did resort to the medical data and talked about how the tests showed there was penetration, and a sperm test matched the sperm of Donny. Bruno smiled and asked that the medical test be examined in some closer detail. He said that vaginal mucosa tests showed no evidence of scarring or torn mucosa, meaning that force was not applied for penetration. The suggestion that was implied was that penetration occurred with an expectation of it. This further implied mutual consent. Donny had turned 18 a month before the encounter, and Penny had turned 18 two weeks before the encounter. This removed the argument of the possibility of a charge of statutory rape. The fact that Penny had disguised herself as a male presenting herself at a male activity raised a suspicion that she was after something other than choir practice. Furthermore Donny's medical exam showed much scarring and teeth marks on his penile appendage. If rape was a question, who raped whom? At this point, the lawyer's brow showed more than a little sweat, and he didn't even try to put his glasses on. The object of his flirtation seemed to lose the pleasure of his advances and showed a curious redness about the eyes and cheeks. She lost all anticipation of a fat reward, to be enjoyed on a trip with her former lawyer friend. Bruno was so bold as to ask the judge what he would do with this case. He paused for a moment then said he'd throw it clear out to the icy cold mountains of Tibet.

Bruno said that he felt that Donny's name had been besmirched by being brought to the court in what appeared to be a contrived scheme and played the tape of the conversation between Donny and Penny. Her advocate screamed that the tape was inadmissible evidence in court, as was much of the testimony. Bruno agreed and added that this was not a court, just a meeting to see which adversarial procedure was most fitting for the case. He then said at the meeting he proposed an out of court settlement of $562,000 for defamation of character. This included court costs and attorney fees. In addition there was the concern that Donny faced expulsion charges and would have his career expectations and acceptance into college colored by the fact that he had to have his private life brought under public scrutiny, with persons that had the discretion to use their powers to accept or reject, according to their subjective attitudes. This was assessed at an additional $700,000. Donny was awarded $1,562,000. It had to be paid over a period of 5 years. The case never got to court. Mictal tried to atone for his role in the affair with Donny, but his advances were met with a Bronx cheer.

The money had to be dealt with sensibly, and then Donny would face the music about his expulsion possibility. Half would go into a savings account, which his father would hold in trust until his 24th birthday; one quarter would go to pay for his school, and the balance would be reinvested. Half of any gains would go back into the savings account, and the other half would be reinvested. If anything should happen to Donny, half of his net worth would go to Becky and any children they had, married or not. Of the remaining assets, the Blackfoot tribe would get a third, his parents would get a third, and Bobby would get a third. In the event something would happen to both parents, Ki would get their third. If one parent survived the parental third would be cut in half, and the remaining monies would be split between Ki and the tribe. Bruno, Corlando and Donny made these decisions together.

Chapter 4

This facet was expected to be a routine slap on the wrist for engaging in sex while under the supervision of both principals. However, the thwarted Ms. Pitressin had other ideas. After Penny got the slap on the wrist, she approached the principal of Phillip Exeter with a substantial donation to the Athletic Department if a certain wrestler was not allowed to darken the doorways of the school. The shame that the mutual consenting act brought to both schools was stressed, especially since a similar endowment was made to Penny's school. Both staffs met together. Then Donny, his father, and the principal of Exeter met. When Corlando heard the expulsion decision, he exploded. "You God damned bastard, you. My son was found innocent of any rape. If their mutual act was so foul, why is only my son punished? The fact that his skin is red, not white isn't connected with it? Is it? Could it also be that the snobby assed Ms. Pitressin cannot tolerate her daughter's holy white skin being soiled by this savage? Well, from what we were able to prove in court, plenty white trash also soiled that and nothing was said. How about that?" Before Ms. Pitressin could respond, Corlando dumped a vase of roses on her head, poured the water from it in her face, while LeBere snatched her lipstick out of her purse, and wrote "asshole" on the desktop with an arrow pointing at the principal. Donny hugged both of his parents and said, "It doesn't matter it's all been phony. At least, while I was here, I taught some preppies to fight back at ugliness with guts, truth, and putting the fear of God into some of their enemies. This has been the first real moment of education I've had at this fine school." He shook hands with the principal and said, "I don't like you very much. To me you're like a preppy that grows up and never learns to challenge the shabby values that make you think you're better than anyone else."

With that done, they walked out arm in arm with their dignity.

Alone, Donny cried at the senseless cruelty he had been victimized by. He was at least able to remember Ki, his father and mother, and Guy Gabaldon, and Ira Hayes. The angry part of him returned. But most of all he remembered Tecumseh.

Donny knew that he'd have to pay his own way by giving his parents rent money until he got his own place. He found a job on the docks of Boston loading and unloading freighters. The thought of stowing away on board one of them kept recurring to him. He stifled it because he didn't want to hurt his parents. He got himself a small used car to get him around and to and from work. He did not want to draw attention as having money and bought a cheap clunker. After all, he had a plan for his money. He was starting to formulate his version of the Pan Indian movement.

As Tecumseh wanted to unite the Amer-Indians culturally and form a bulwark against the white man, Donny sought to use the whites' weaknesses to create a path to cultural unity in a way similar to the way that the white man had brought a foreign substance (alcohol) to the Indians, poisoned their bodies with it, and then blamed the Red man for having a weakness for the substance, so would he bring the Caucasian down. After mentally scanning the makeup of the pale intruder to his land, the Blackfoot came up with a plan: He knew from his experiences in the dorm that wanting something for nothing was an almost universal trait amongst the whites, as well as all men. He also knew the desperation in which most tribal cultures were living. Hence, he deduced that if he could convince the tribal elders to pursue his plan of cashing in on whitey's greed to produce an income for themselves, the way many white bartenders had cashed in on the weakness for the alcohol they had introduced to his people, both a stable income could be produced, and means of bringing down the predator could be achieved. When he met with lonely, defeated tribesmen in bars, he encouraged them to arrange meetings with these elders and discussed their pushing to get ownership of casinos in their geographic areas. He also let them know that money would be available to negotiate the purchases, but he did not mention the sources.

Becky and his father had tried to warn him that one did not achieve good results by practicing evil ways, but his answer always was to draw their attentions to the sweet words followed by foul deeds of the cultural enemy. It was they, not he that had chosen the battle plan and battleground.

One day, he passed Mictal and Penny Pitressin crossing the street to get to their schools. He stopped the car and said hello to them. Mictal was reticent to talk to him after his insincere attempts at friendliness were snubbed. But Penny was glad to see him. She smiled sadly and told Donny that she had left her mother's house because she could not stand being a part of her scheme, especially using the endowments to the school as a wedge to deprive Donny of the rest of his education. Donny indicated to her that this was all water over the dam; in all actuality it was: for here he was thrown into the world of manhood, while these two were still struggling to find out who they would become. He politely excused himself from this conversation and advised them that he did not want to be late for work. Her sad and longing look followed him to the car.

That night while he was at home, pangs of conscience nagged at him. He wrote a letter to Becky recounting the day's events and the feelings that it generated. He knew his feelings for vengeance were justified, but he also recalled the feelings of kindness and forgiveness that his parents, Ki, and the Mikawbers had tried to teach him. Was he Cain, seeking out Abel, to kill for his own purposes? Or was he trying to identify with the aggressive white man to tell him that the Red Man can also be an aggressor if the shoe was on the other foot? Which position had the groundwork of moral rectitude behind it? What's more would Becky's feelings for him be tarnished by the path he was considering going on? These concepts tore at his mind. He had to take a respite in his life and sort out his ideas on the subject. He decided to go to his two mentors to find the answers. Maybe he'd find the answers in their words.

Ki was digging in a flower bed when Donny encountered him. He presented his dilemma. The oriental with wisdom the lad sought tried to be neutral in what he said because Donny was a boy on the brink of manhood and could be vulnerable. He reminded him about how the

Jewish soldier had befriended him: how he turned the three German boys into friends so long ago, and how Moses Doleman took on the bullies that were after him. He confessed to the lad that putting hatreds aside for the betterment of all of humanity taught a valuable lesson, but most people often return to the culture that spawned them and re-adapted to the ways that had meant survival to them and abandoned altruism. Yet a culture built on hatred does not last because wiping out or weakening another group leaves the same bloodlust and enemies that are ineffective or gone, and the survivors turn on each other because they have the same inner needs and the same outer targets. He said that we can't give out constant charity because others, with greed in their hearts, will turn on us. We have to balance this out with healing ourselves so that we do not create malice and contribute to our own destruction.

Donny went into the house and saw Becky and his father engrossed in a game of backgammon. They looked up when they saw him come in with a look of puzzled concern on his face. He opened up about what was bothering him and what Ki had proposed as a solution. Corlando had to pause and think a minute, and Becky took up the slack in the interval. She reminded him that even Tecumseh wanted to create a culture that could act as a broker in the fashion that was suggested by James Baldwin. He knew the fallacy of trying to crush the whites; they would be up against more money and more destructive weaponry. To hit the white man where he was weak would not only expose vulnerability but would engender hatred, hatred that had a framework of more advanced technology geared for war. This would be the start of a slaughter, not a Pan Indian culture. Corlando had interjected that both she and Ki had a point in avoiding the self destruction that tearing someone down would only lead to an anger that would motivate unification to repeat the behavior that had brought the Indian to the minority and victim status. To be a broker, one had to have something the other party wanted enough to force dealings on an equal plain. Donny got the message, but he applied the principle to the wanting something for nothing as a necessary part of the white character. This was not so in all instances. He advised his mentors that he would have to try his way, if for no other reason, the Red Man had to equalize the economic disadvantage to begin to function as a broker. Every ethnic white gang leader used this manner of gaining a foothold into the economy to advance the group from a minority status. Al Capone did it; Arnold Rothstein did it. Corlando sadly shook his head and said, "I'll love you always forever, but you're going to have to experience the pain that your way brings to learn what you have to do." Becky agreed to stand by his side and help to pick up the pieces when they fell. He had already proven that he loved her; all that she could do was stand by her man.

Donny was haunted by dreams that night. He had visions of Ki, his father, and Becky pointing their fingers at him calling out, "Where has Donny gone, Long time passing; Long time ago; gone to a soldier, all of him; Gone to the graveyard, all of him." This was the cost of his decision to go to war.

He worked for two years on the docks; with every ship he loaded the pressure to leave grew inside him. He wanted to take Becky with him and leave the country that had proven to be built on a pack of lies to him, but he felt a sense of loyalty to all who loved him; it held him back from his resolve. What nagged at him was the conflict that he saw in the society and in himself for the ones who had loved him and whom he had loved. He felt he could not separate himself from his feelings for his loved ones when he thought of revenge against the defilers of the simple ways of the tribe, and the simple folkways that looked to these explanatory beliefs became hollow once the white man appeared on their shores with his deceit and his guns. A peaceful co-existence between Man and his world of nature when the gods were formulated to be the ultimate cause of the natural phenomena was disrupted. What replaced it was the ugly desolation and hopelessness of the reservation. These kinds of thoughts brought him to the point of blind rage.

Becky could see the troubled thoughts racing through his mind. She would take his hand and lead him to a quiet place. Then she would draw him to her and kiss him gently. She would talk of the goodness of Corlando and LeBere, and the impossibility of his maintaining views of racial hatred amidst the love they all had for him. She also reminded him that Bobby was thriving in this environment and would be able to find justice without the destructiveness that tore into Donny's soul. She began to fool with the buttons on his shirt and stroke his chest. She would snuggle against him and reach for his manhood while he began to disrobe her. They kissed and touched each other all over in the simple beauty of their nakedness until neither one could stand the separation between them. She pulled him to her and asked him to enter her. They moved, at first slowly and gently, until she whispered into his ear, "Do it to me." With a grin on his lips, he asked her, "Do what?" She bit his ear and he began to move harder and faster until her heart began to quiver. They moaned together and reached the high point of their union. Afterwards they lay together arm in arm and snuggled. Donny sighed and said to Becky that he couldn't stand to be pulled in two directions. He felt that he had to leave to make up his mind which way he had to go. He was going to join the Merchant Marines and search his soul. Becky became saddened and said she'd wait for him and would stay with him either way. He kissed her gratefully and said to himself that he didn't deserve this kind of love.

The next day, while he still had the resolve, he signed up for the Merchant Marines. He left the country two weeks later. The time at sea was lonely and hard. He tried not to make too many friends because he did not like the idea of getting close to someone and then departing from them with the painful feeling that there was no more. He missed Becky terribly and wrote her when he could. He would visit bookstores and pawn shops while on leave and never missed an opportunity to buy a trinket or book of poetry or a novel for her and send it to her. Her letters were getting scanter, and ill at ease; suspiciously, he began to ask Bobby and others to whom he wrote if they had noticed any difference in her. They were equally silent. He had a leave coming and resolved to discover for himself to see what had changed. He had leave in the port of Boston and would not let anyone know that he was home. He found out that Becky was pregnant and didn't want him to worry about her and that she was being besieged with offers of marriage, which she was resisting.

While at home he got a letter from the Reservation from someone called Boar's Tusk, asking for help in paying the asking price for a gambling establishment right on the border of Upper Peninsula and

Ontario. They were asking $275,500 for it. He flew there and negotiated with Boar's Tusk and the current owners. The Blackfoot tribe would own 48% of the stock, and he would own 52%. Of this, 26% was to be invested and Becky was to receive all income from the investment and own 26%. He then wrote his broker of these instructions and a letter, informing Becky of what he had done and proposing marriage by the beginning of the summer with an emerald ring and necklace enclosed. What he didn't tell her was that he had left instructions with Boar's Tusk to keep him informed of the clientele and their winnings and losses every month. He wanted to be able to select which clients got encouragement/discouragement and clamping down procedures for payment of markers. He also purchased a boat casino on the Mississippi between Texas and Louisiana. Boar's Tusk was the manager of both casinos, and the instruction pattern was the same, as was the income distribution.

When he was back aboard ship, he found a letter from Becky accepting his proposal and stating that she was ecstatic about the ring, accompanied by a letter from his parents, full of love and congratulations but also stating that they hoped he had resolved his dilemma about revenge. He knew that the uncertainty about his having reached a solution came from his father and/or Ki. He smiled to himself, but the smile was not one of happiness.

Most of Donny's assignments were rather innocuous cargo deliveries, but the last assignment he was to have was fraught with excitement and danger. His captain was given the assignment of breaking up a liaison between a group of headhunters and a ring of pirates in the Pacific Islands near the site of Iwo Jima. The island was near enough to Iwo Jima to have been part of the battle site. In fact, it was riddled with tunnels from the Japanese occupation. The pirates turned out to be a Japanese submarine crew that had not surrendered and did not know that the war was over. They had propagandized the natives to believe that the whites only had imperialistic desires on the island. Hence they had banded together to defend the island. The island was mined from the beaches to the mountains where the tunnels ended. Wild boars, tigers, and mountain lions constituted the wildlife of the island. They were all carnivorous, and meats from the ship were placed near the headhunter village. As animals were drawn to the scent and aggregated at the periphery of the village, a fire was lit behind them and spread to the brush, also behind them, driving them into the village to provoke the headhunters into fighting the animals. Those that sought escape encountered the land mines. At the same time, part of the crew went into the tunnels and fired guns, which echoed to create the impression of many more than they were. As they ran out, they encountered the fires, the land mines, and the ship firing at them. A path was cleared to allow them to get to their beached submarine of which they took advantage. They were quickly out to sea. The headhunters, seeing that their friends had deserted them sulkily returned to their village and began the business of repair. Donny, who had devised the strategy of using the animals that inhabited the island and the property of hollow chambers to produce echoes was given a commendation. Now he was ready to go home and be a father and husband.

Donny was ready to wed. His parents, the Mikawbers/Dolemans, the La Mondes, Ki, his friends from the dorm, Penny without her mother, and Mictal were invited. Craine was surprised that there was still an Ornam alive, but he found out that the family had emigrated from Ireland before he was born. Still he felt impelled to tell Donny not to trust Mictal too much. Donny answered that he already knew this and kept him close enough to him to watch him and nothing else. Craine smiled and could see that he was talking to a smart little soldier. The couple shared their vows with each other. Donny vowed that whatever befell him, nothing would touch Becky or their children; for he would protect them from the God of winds and the God that blotted out the sunlight, as well as any harbinger of sickness, pain or death. He swore this by the Gods that had raised him to manhood. Becky vowed that she would be the mother of his children and his childish errors of thought for as long as there was a Mother Earth, that the cold of the North Wind would never touch him, that she would bring motherly protection over him and all their children. Ki caught her garter, and Bobby caught her bouquet and gave it to the nearest single girl he could find. He caught it because it had a thorny stem and was about to land on his eye. Their honeymoon was in Quebec City, and they made passionate love for four hours on the Plains of Abraham. Lonely Otter's ghost probably smiled that the useful part of Man's function was returned to a Native Canadian after the French and British slaughtered one another to see who was smart enough to rule them, and neither one was. Perhaps the beaver I saw in that park also got an eyeful of the merriment.

Donny had to finish his hitch in the Merchant Marines, which was another 6 months. The task that was given to the crew was to rescue an American family from Port Arthur, a city in Manchuria near the Russian border, where the Russians were defeated by the Japanese in 1905, and where there was a massacre in the Sino-Japanese War. The family was missionaries. The ship docked at the port, and three men were sent as reconnaissance to assess the strength and to come up with a plan to get the family out. Donny was one of the men, as was a former French Foreign Legionnaire, and an escapee from a Turkish Prison with a drug record. They had resolved among themselves to perform the rescue themselves. They were disguised as antique dealers looking for rugs and carpets. They had located the family in their former church with communist guards all around the building. The plan to get into the building was to bring four rolled up carpets in a truck to sell to the church, wrap up the boy, girl, man, and wife in a carpet and carry them out, while feigning an argument with the church officials, who supposedly refused to buy their wares. The scheme entailed a conference with the church elders and priest and the family and a means of disabling the guards. This involved sneaking into the church while the guards were asleep late at night and planning to put drugs that would induce sleep into their food and/or drink. The drug user mixed vicodan with trazodone, a sleeping pill and put it into a soup the guards drank, as well as into their coffee cups. The zero hour was at four P.M. when people become sleepy from their lunches.

The three raiders walked past the doped up guards with their carpets and demanded from the guard inside to see the Robinsons. They had an important transaction to conduct with them. The half awake soldier directed them to the left to the quarters of the prisoners. Once inside, the rugs were unrolled; each family member was assigned a rug to lie down on. The rugs were rolled up onto a cart, and the cart was wheeled out to a truck. The truck had the belongings of the Robinsons, which had been secreted aboard late the previous night. Inside each rug was an oxygen tank attached to a hose through which the rolled up person breathed while in storage. The truck drove down to the pier, where the ship was docked. A Manchurian guard that was not drugged stopped them at the dock and wanted to see what was inside the rugs. The Legionnaire was the first one stopped. He laid the rolled up rug down on the pier and faced the Marxian policeman. Donny knelt behind him, and when he was pushed over him, Donny seized a rock and crushed his head then threw him in the water to allow the recovered addict to emerge from under the dock to snap his neck. With the disposal having taken place, the four bundles were brought on board the ship. Once they were outside the range of Port Arthur, the Robinsons emerged from their rug rolls. The captain came out smiling and said, "I guess we can sit down together and come up with a plan to smuggle them out of there, now that the scouts are back."

The shipmates decided to have a farewell party for Donny and took him to a strip joint. The stripper became enamored with Donny's dark good looks and decided to snuggle with him and pick his pocket. At the end of the evening, she kissed him goodbye and handed him back his wallet and watch. He was surprised at her skill and very embarrassedly handed her back her panties and nipple caps. She was shocked and asked, "How did you get them without my feeling anything?" Donny smiled mysteriously and said that he had bought them from the stripper next to her in the dressing room between acts. The girl protested that she did not know what color undergarments that she wore, and he said that he did because he had been there before. He also said that over garments was a more accurate description. She said that she had never seen him before. His answer was that he had come there to see her, not to be seen by her. He added that he liked what he saw and smiled seductively. She shook her finger at him and laughed. Then he went home to his wife, now in Boston looking for a house.

Chapter 5

The resurrector of Tecumseh's cultural plan took his position as the hidden director of the Upper Peninsula gambling establishment by inventing a unique name for it. He suggested the name, The Diced Chick. He knew well some of his enemies and friends' proclivities and brought them into his establishment, under the guise of an interview by Boar's Tusk, people that had management skills coupled with destructive something for nothing drives, that served as the parent of an addictive personality that could be drawn out by the presence of the gambling machine that lay under their greed. For this reason he made sure that enticing literature found its way to Ms. Pitressin, but not Penny, Mictal, Ornam, the Principal of Phillip Exeter Academy, some of the bullies he and Bobby had encountered in their stormy boyhood in Fargo. Likewise, he kept his brother and parents, Becky, Ki, the Mikawbers/Dolemans, and La Mondes away from any connection with gambling, but he forgot he was only a self-appointed god over peoples' lives and did not control the directions that these lives always took. Whatever good came of lives was interspersed with less than good motives. Only the person imbued with the good or evil can direct these paths. The amount of discipline and/or relation to the Godhead are the factors that direct outcomes, not the manipulations of mortals.

The first lesson came when Donny got a call from Rodin explaining that his son, Randal, was picking up a gambling habit and was hanging around with some dangerous folks that were making him a victim of loan sharks. He had contacted Craine, who subdued the cronies the same way Donny had been subdued by former pimps and gamblers. However the portion of the problem that remained was that he had lost money in Montreal and had left himself vulnerable to the sharks and had to wire his dad to send him money to get home which he was about to gamble away at The Diced Chick. Donny also learned by observation that one of the loan shark's underlings had seen Randal and was about to get his hooks into him. He had Mictal, who worked for him as a croupier, watch them both and to rig their first game so they won, but all their other games so that they lost a substantial amount of money, then call in their markers and send them individually to him.

Donny preserved his identity by wearing a mask and using a trick microphone to disguise his voice. He had Rodin fax a picture of Randal's girlfriend and their baby to him. He confronted Randal with the pictures, as well as showing him pictures of other girlfriends after the loan sharks had gotten a hold of them. He showed him the $900,000 debt he had built up and told him that he knew his father well and would be checking with him to make sure he was going to Gamblers Anonymous 5 times a week and keeping his nose clean. If he did this and did not gamble, the $900,000 would be forgiven. If he did not go or gambled, it would fall due in its entirety with consequences that the pictures showed, done to him, not the girl or child. The girl and child would be moved to another area and their names changed. If he tried to find them, again he would receive the expected consequences, as had been portrayed.

The loan shark's playmate was also handled in an unusual disciplinary measure. He had been under an alias. He had to make his $900,000 debt good and did go through his old boss under the alias he had assumed so that he would be treated as any other debtor by the shark. Failure at compliance or attempts to reveal his actual identity or otherwise seek a softening of the blow would end up with a brand new pair of cement shoes.

Mictal was recruited to reduce his arrogance to subservience. His habit was used to victimize him into a huge debt then canceling it in return for loyal service. If the service was in any way disloyal, he was shown films of the four men in the rescue team and would be offered the reward of their dismantlement skills as a benefit for it.

There were several choices to be made that decided whether he was a kind or an avenging angel of God, but the pregnancy of Becky brought him down to the position of a man that loved his family.

Becky was irresistible to him. Every time she bent over or nudged him, he was upon her. She never had her bedclothes on for long. Mornings she was so sore that she could not get up without agony to make breakfast. She found this humorous and joked with Donny about it only hurting when she laughed. When her water broke, they were in a friend's pool playing water polo. Donny was carrying her on his shoulders when it happened. She was rushed to the hospital in her bathing suit, and he in one that was too large for him that was the same style as his that he had accidentally picked up. While she was on the gurney, he had to hold her hand with one hand and keep pulling up his trunks with the other. After 16 hours of labor, Becky had twins with dark eyes and dark hair. The only problem was one was a boy, and one was a girl. They named the girl Ambler and the boy Rambler. Immediately after the birth, a third zygote appeared. It turned out to be a boy, who was named, Gambler. He proved to be the apple of his father's eye. Donny was happy to return to chasing Becky around the house and trying to undress her at inopportune times, such as when she was washing clothes or brushing her teeth.

There were two more people on Donny's vengeance list and another reward. He had happened upon Penny Pitressin in Tijuana while on vacation with his family. He was out for a morning jog when an attractive leg barred his path, and a cutesy voice said, "How about it big boy." He answered that he was a happily married man, and she said, "I'll never tell if you don't." He said to pay him, and he'd think about it. She looked up at that point, and so did he. They recognized each other. They sat down at a cafe and exchanged greetings and brought one another up to date. Penny's mother and the principal, who expelled Donny had gotten friendly, and he had made arrangements with her principal to send Penny to school tuition and housing free via a scholarship. Ms. Pitressin invested the money she had set aside for Penny's school fees in a dress shop that sold to an exclusive set of women in a suburb in Boston. It was part of a chain, and she opened up an additional shop in suburban L.A. and had Penny move out there to manage the store. She found out that Orange County was planning a highway through there and sold it and the land around it to the county displacing her daughter from her management position. Penny tried to get a job to be able to maintain the plush condo she had bought for a year. She was not prepared with sufficient skills, and her mother refused to finance any more schools or lend her any money. As a consequence, she started working in strip joints and discovered that men wanted the real thing, not a show, when a sailor that came to see her waited in the wings of the theater and took her in the alley next door and raped her. She got pregnant and had to support both of them. She started turning tricks. In the meantime the principal had followed what Ms. Pitressin was doing with the capital gains she had acquired and invested his money in the highway that Orange County was building, as well as investing in the initial store in Boston.

The gambler wanted to capitalize on their greed in a single stroke. He thought the best way to do this was to reduce them to a couple and make Penny's reward contingent on their being pulled into a downfall by their greed as a couple. He started the ball rolling by mailing romantic notes from one to the other and getting them to set up a date via these letters to one another. He set up a seminar for businessmen to find ways to avoid certain taxes and donated funds to a local university to put it on. He mailed an advertisement of it to both of them. The principal phoned Ms. Pitressin and asked her to accompany him to the function. She was exuberant about the invitation. Donny also attended it to be sure that they were there. He also sponsored a raffle in which the winning ticket holder won a free evening at The Diced Chick and rigged it so that they would win. Thus, he had begun to tap into their something for nothing mentalities. The club owner watched their expressions of greed by starting them out as big winners to get their greed juices flowing.

He let them have their so-called winning streak long enough to glean a marriage proposal and the new couple's investing in a huge mansion together. At this point, Donny pulled out the stops and introduced, first, smaller winning streaks, then small losses that seemed to increase. This was followed by advice from their stockbroker, who was Mictal, to make certain investments controlled by Donny that would make a profit then get sold suddenly then plummet in value. They would gamble more to cover their losses. When they reached a point at which their collective marker was not acceptable, they were brought before the masked owner with the funny voice. He put a lien on their house which they could not meet, as well as the Boston store. The manager who worked there became the owner's employee, and the couple was thrown out in the cold. Donny found them an apartment in the inner city with a business opportunity owning a newsstand, which they could develop with their own industry. He informed Penny that she now had a house and business in Boston with a capable manager for as long as she wanted it. He also said he'd buy them each from her if she wanted to get rid of them. She sold the house to him but kept the business. Donny rented the house out and put it in Becky's name so that she would have an income without working and could raise their three children properly. When she heard this news, he did not have to chase her around the house or coax her into amorous activity.

The world is not always your oyster. Donny had some bad news from home. His father was in a plane crash, and his legs were crushed. His ability to walk again was doubtful. He was brought to Mother Mary's Hospital. He left Boar's Tusk in charge of the casino and hurried home to find out what he could do to help. He saw Rodin, Craine, Patrick and his wife and family there. LeBere was full of fear and shaking. He went to her immediately and put his arm around her. Becky and the little ones did the same. He wondered if this was God's way of paying him back for the cruel way in which he was manipulating people's lives and resolved to talk with Ki about it. Bobby rushed in from his law school finals and started to fall apart. He left his mother to the ministrations of Becky and went to his brother. He hugged Bobby to him and let him cry on his shoulder, the way he used to do in Fargo. Bobby snapped out of it and went to help his mother.

The news was not good. Corlando's legs did not have to be amputated, but there was permanent nerve damage to the lumbar area and a kidney was injured. He would be confined to a wheelchair and might need a transplant. Both boys volunteered, along with Ki, but they were rejected because of the racial differences.

Donors were coming out of the woodwork. Mictal and Penny had volunteered but were rejected. Patrick and Craine, Rodin and Randal, the females in all of the families were rejected. Donny was told that he had to get a kidney in three weeks or Corlando was done for. In desperation, Donny got the phenotype, genotype blood type needed from the doctor and sent Bobby, his mother, and his wife to the drivers' license bureaus to find volunteer donors and check out the paperwork, while he started calling transplant agencies to locate possible donors. There was no luck anywhere. Another brainstorm hit him. He went to ER's to locate unclaimed bodies from accidents or violent deaths. He hit pay dirt and made arrangements for immediate transport of freshly removed kidneys.

Surgery was done the next day; Donny's dad survived the surgery and lived another 15 years due to it.

Inadvertently, Donny found out that the kidney he received was a black market kidney. When the director of the foundation proved to be the loan shark with whom Randal had dealt, and he tried to shake the Blackfoot down, he got an education. He called Donny in for a meeting to decide what kind of fee or favor would be owed. Three hours later the black marketer was seen slumped over his desk with a Tomahawk in his forehead. Several soldiers were sent to find Donny, and they were all found in a similar condition.

When Donny got home Becky threw her arms around him and proclaimed him as her hero. He grinned and said, "I expect my reward upstairs." She laughed and said, "I'm not in the mood. You better take a cold shower." He reached inside her blouse and suggested a cold shower together. They raced to the bathtub, and she was the first to take her clothes off. Once the water was on, he began to kiss her thighs and her labia and to tongue her lovingly. She began to groan and to scream, "Yes, yes. YES, more, more." She grabbed his tumescence and could feel it swell. She began to pull it to her and moaned as she put him inside her. He began to penetrate deeper and deeper until he could go no further. Then he began to scream and to rock. She perpetuated his motion and began to moan, "Deeper, faster, harder." 'Their juices began to flow and to mingle. They began to rock harder and faster until they reached a crescendo and they reached their peak together. Afterward, they fell asleep in each others' arms unaware that a pair of alien eyes was watching them. They had been watching them for several days. The eyes belonged to someone that was higher in power than a soldier. In fact they belonged to Don Enrico Dombrero, of the Hispanic Brotherhood. He was perturbed because problems were beginning to emerge in some of his loan shark and black market organ donor markets. Now that he had pinpointed Donny's weakness, he only had to plug in the right gimmick that would trigger Donny's fear for his family The Don chose making Donny part of his activity as a task of debt to be repaid to him for his part in neutralizing the loan shaking business and for getting a free kidney for his father from him. Needless to say he had infiltrated the gambling enterprise if he knew Donny headed it. Donny wondered what else he knew about him.

Chapter 6

Enrico Dombrero grew up as the 14th child of the local communist leader in the town of Tijuana. There was a lot of anti-American feeling in the town because of the availability of prostitutes to Gringos from California and Texas. Such a large family would normally put this family into the dungeon of poverty, except that a connection had been established between a drug growing family in the Andes Mountains that grew both the opium poppy and the cocaine plant, the Ruozo family. Enrico hated his father. Doctrine was pushed at him to point of his not being allowed to eat dinner if he disagreed with his father's politics. If he wanted to play soccer after school, he had to forego the pleasure because working for the freedom of the peasants from Yankee imperialism was more important than having fun, which was regarded as a waste of time. Enrico's mother had died at the age of 37 from stomach cancer. Enterboam Dombrero, the family's paternal figure, could not cope with his wife's pain and sought a scapegoat amongst his children and one to make into his image so that he could glorify his sacrifice of his children to the struggle for the liberation of the Mexican peasant from imperialism. He had witnessed the heroic manner in which Josef Stalin eliminated his enemies and mobilized the Russians at Stalingrad to kick Hitler out of Russia. Hence, his family felt like a Stalinist cell, not a family. He left the agitation and the lust for revenge for his own criminal empire. This empire would now be enhanced and built by forcing Donny Clippingbird into its axis of power.

The final blow came when Enterboam began to belittle his son and to make fun of him in public and to stop beating him and use psychological torture tactics to make him submit to his will. Enrico warned his father to desist from these tactics, and when he refused,

Enrico took off his shoe and beat him with it until he drew blood. He then kicked off his other shoe, told his father to insert his entire house in his posterior region, walked out, and sought out the local Mafia chieftain to liberate the Mexican proletariat of their pesos and of gringos by sending them home in body bags.

Don Dombrero had soldati follow the family to learn who their friends were, what their schedules were, and times and places they were vulnerable. He wanted to get the whole family at one crack and reasoned that the best time was at 1:30, when the little ones were awakened from their naps, and Becky had just returned from grocery shopping.

Becky noticed a couple men following her for a couple days, but she paid it no mind, figuring they had just moved into the neighborhood. Today when she finished her shopping and went to her car, she felt a gloved hand clamp on her mouth and nose with a cloth on it and lost consciousness. A woman about Becky's size and shape, came to her car and changed clothes with her The car was driven to her house. The woman, who favored Becky from a distance used the house keys on the ring to get in the house and bring Ambler, Rambler, and Gambler down into a waiting car. Next she got back into Becky's car and followed the other one to an abandoned factory that held a helicopter at a spot directly under a skylight. That night when Donny came home from work, he found a note that stated:

> If you want to see your family intact again I suggest you give me $5,000,000 to cover my losses that occurred because you caused a crimp In my loan sharking, which caused me to have to kill one of my best men in that business. You also had the gall (yuk, yuk) to steal a kidney from my Organ Transplant gig. I want the money within three weeks. Going to the cops won't do you any good. I own them and the judges that would be involved in this matter.
>   Your friend,
>   Don Enrico Dombrero
>
> P.S. I will also need the assistance of Mr. Patrick Mikawber and yourself in a special project I have planned. I'll see you in my

office next Thursday to discuss our arrangements. I bet this is the first ransom note you saw with a joke in it.

Donny sat down on the bed and wept. Then he got up mad. He phoned Ki, the Mikawber/Dolemans, the La Mondes, Boar's Tusk, Mictal, his parents and Bobby, and any federal, state or local officials that owed him a favor; he read them the contents of the note. Then he said, "I have loved you, and you have loved me. Now I want you to help me develop a plan to help me bring my family back to me and to fix this little bastard so that he never messes with anyone in our families again."

Craine and his family nosed around the gangland back alleys and found that the Don's story was true. They also smoked out the soldiers responsible for the death of the loan shark, and began tailing them to see what information they had to impart. Some phone tapping also entered into the picture. Boar's Tusk was given the assignment to find out who the "industrial spy" at The Diced Chick was. Donny had figured that someone had to be working with the Don from inside, or no one would have known that he was in charge and that the loan shark was an object of punishment.

Three days of eavesdropping on the tapped phone of the soldiers led to Donny's recognizing the voice of the lady involved in abducting his family. Her name was Scherlien Dotson. She worked as a singer and dealer at the blackjack table. She was from Ann Arbor, Michigan and was interested in the history of the Purple Gang. She began dating gangsters at 18 years of age because she wanted to be where the fast money was. She had gambling experience in Atlantic City where she met the loan shark and let him know she was available to him in return for introductions to the "big boys." From there she paved her own road. After she had cultivated the interest of Enrico Dombrero, he gave her the assignment to find out what was going on at that new casino that had opened up in Upper Michigan, The Diced Chick.

Apparently, she had learned how to get men to give up information because Enrico was able to learn about who the head honcho there was and that one of his lieutenants was not careful about the tactics his men used finding suckers. The families met and decided to make use of the fear element. Since the two men that were being tailed had communications and saw themselves as sophisticates that brought what the ignorant wanted for themselves for high stakes, and Scherlien saw herself as too smart and slick to work for a living, information was circulated about a shipment of emeralds and diamonds that were located in a store (rented by the mob) under light guard with an electronic beam as the only protection against robbery for purposes of testing the effectiveness of the beam. Donny could see with his mind's eye the greedy plans developing and the process of learning the lay of the land. In fact, he was able to predict when they would try their caper. He had fishing nets hung from the ceiling that were laced with chloroform, laced with cocaine. This was the formulary for the initial capture. It worked like a charm.

The second phase involved using fear of the red man's savagery. After the capture all three were blindfolded, and their clothes were taken away while they were unconscious. They were placed in a pot of cold water, scrubbed clean with huge brushes from a car wash, put back in a pot of warm water to which "spices" were added. These were ground up hair from a barbershop, rust from a ship's anchor, the juice from a tobacco chaw, and ground up asphalt. To further create the illusion of cannibals preparing a meal, a troop of actors that played Indians in westerns danced around the kettle and made whatever weird sounds came to their minds; they would periodically sample the taste of the elixir and add or take away "spices" to the abominable brew. The only one that was to be affected was Scherlien. Her hair was also stroked by several of the dancers.

She broke, as predicted, and could not wait to tell her interrogators where Becky and the children were stashed. She never did figure out why she was not fired; the reason was that she was germane to the clean up operation: She was in the vicinity when she overheard Donny and Boar's Tusk whispering about breaking into the factory and rescuing the family at midnight four days away. In two days McTavish and Tyndall Mikawber rescued the family and blew the helicopter to smithereens while Patrick and Donny were in Mexico to pick up the drug shipment from the Ruozo family. Instead they bombed the drug processing lab and flew to the Andes and sprayed a combination of skunk spray extract, DDT, and stinkweed extract on the poppy and cocaine fields, as well as the newly built villa that the Ruozos had built. Then they got the hell out of there.

Needless to say, a contract was put out on Patrick and Donny. They abrogated it by abrogating Don Enrico in the following manner. They broke into his palatial home by cutting through the sewer system and found him asleep with his current mistress, both of them in the raw. With a huge pastry brush, they brushed them with honey and placed three hornets nests in the bed at the levels of their genitalia and heads then turned loose a very affectionate bear cub. The cub began licking Don Enrico and became more interested once he tasted the honey; with the motion came a jarring of the hornets' nest at the head of the bed. The Don's movement in response caused him to turn over, thinking his playmate was getting frisky. This jarred the nest at the level of his genitalia. Then he screamed at the aspect of dealing with a bear cub and two nests full of hornets. He ran away and jumped out of the window three stories from the ground and broke his neck. They stopped the paramour and got her out of there since they had had no dealings with her. The rest of the family became too involved in the war of succession to bother with the enforcement of the contract. Donny was ready to return to the waiting arms of his family. Corlando was well on the road to recovery. The power of the Ruozos was broken in the countries of the Andes, and another lieutenant tried to substitute himself in their position. He had been a liaison between the Andes corporation and the United States. His name was Tandry Obrits. He didn't like having animals for shipmates or the cold of Switzerland. He stowed away on a boat that went to Nicaragua and made the connection with the Ruozo family. Now he found himself unemployed with two big sources and his American outlet for the product destroyed. He knew that he had to deal with that sheenie loving Mikawber bunch, as well as their Frog and Redskin buddies. He knew that they were too thick as friends to let one of them get hurt. He decided to get them at the level of what they did for a living. There was Patrick's airline, Craine's and Rodin's trucking firm, and Donny's gambling establishment. He had an inside track to Donny's business: Mictal Ornam. He intended to make contact with his family members in the Senate and House of Representatives. He used loyalty to Erin and the IRA to get through to him.

Mictal had no illusions about why Donny had put him in a high position at The Diced Chick, but his voluntarism in the area of being willing to donate a kidney for Corlando somehow touched both him and Donny and created the idea that perhaps they shared a real friendship through the years they had known each other. This feeling of relationship was soon placed in the realm of a deep and basic testing.

Mictal had not maintained contact with the auld Irish branch of the family. In fact his only connection was Uncle Tandry, who wasn't really an uncle. He was surprised at the invitation to lunch, and was only too happy to attend until he found out the true nature of the appointment. His uncle went into a tirade about Jew and Jap lovers along with treating Redskins as if they were anything but savages running around the country bare arsed and running things they had no business getting into. He offered to set this nation right and take away the assumed rights of these minority creeps, who were leading the country to wrack and ruin with their inferiority and ineptitude. Mictal, who had always thought of Tandry as a harmless old man trying to bring back the good old days when Irishmen were the underdog fighting for their own recognition, became alarmed at what he was hearing. He wanted to relay it to Donny, but he also wanted to understand what was going on.

He got taken through Craine's war with the family, beginning with his and McTavish's interest in establishing a union, the Ornams' attempt to bring the Mikawbers into the fold of God Fearing Catholic Irishmen and enduring to their mingling with damn Jews that were part of their scheme to take over the world by dividing Christian souls. He cried over poor Jesse slain after he got on the boat for New Zealand, as well as the fatal bombing of the Ornams. He went on to attack Craine's association with hoodlums then switched to the traitor Frog that played his country at both ends to sell them out to anti-war commies in the years of the Vietnamese war, not to mention the Redskin that was breaking self respecting white men with his whorish gambling establishment. He put the question to Mictal: Did he want this rot to continue or did he want to stand shoulder to shoulder with white men who respected freedom and dignity?

Mictal had learned enough about human nature to realize that regardless of where his friends and predecessors had stood, their hearts were always in the right place. He thought about how he had once tried to make Donny a victim in a sucker's game and how he tried to play God, he was not cruel and backward and tried to be fair to others. He remembered how Donny had taught him how to fight the drunks that attempted to roll him instead of running to ineffective authorities.

Tandry was able to deduce that Mictal was more loyal to his friends than he was to relatives that he never knew. In fact, he went to Craine, Rodin, and Donny immediately with the plot that Tandry was hatching almost at the same time that Tandry was approaching the Senator and Representative. They decided to call a meeting. Their conclusion was that they would fight fire with fire. They resolved to hire a private eye to dig up dirt on Tandry then turn it over to a lawyer to present a case to the Civil Liberties Union for harassment and invasion of privacy. This was to be used as a lever to get Tandry to choose between deportation and standing trial for a very high lawsuit.

Craine and Rodin had an advantage over Donny in their age bracket because there were not any witnesses left to testify, and they had covered their tracks so that no one could testify that they were the ones that had perpetrated the acts. They also had the benefit of sympathy for the causes in which the acts were perpetrated, such as fighting the depression and fighting for an allied victory to the war. However, Donny had the advantage of fighting for the rights of a minority by vengeance and having helped a spoiled group of preppies learn to defend themselves from criminal assault. He also hurt people that had hurt him.

The legal brains that organized the case against Tandry were Bruno Havelich and Bobby. Through Moses they discovered that Tandry was a Neo Nazi. He had found a membership card with his name on it the day they rescued Ki. Further examination implicated him in several incidents of brutalizing Blacks during civil rights demonstrations. They were backed up by photographs. He was also implicated in a stand off of the government in Oregon, and a witness had made a statement that he was there with him that was also verified by a photo. When the Congressmen summoned them to a meeting, the evidence was presented. It was also sent to the Civil Liberties Union. The end result was that Tandry was given a choice between deportation to Ireland or facing a $150,000 lawsuit if he fought it. Shaking his fist at Mictal and vowing revenge, he got on the boat for Dublin.

The upshot of this series of events showed the three of them that the time was coming to clean up their acts. They were engaged in sponsoring group homes for kids from troubled families and finding family therapists for them and finding umbrellified services for the community's homeless that had metropolitan housing working with vocational rehab agencies to create independence. This did still seem to leave a vacuum in the feeling of wholeness. At a meeting of Gamblers Anonymous, Rodin heard the doctrine that forgiveness is for the forgiver because it frees a person from maintaining a position of hatred that is so self-destructive and stops a person from changing into the person he/she wants to be by clinging to past issues.

The journey to self introspection brought a look at how a gigantic slaughter had impelled men to look at their destructive and protective behavior patterns that came to the fore to maintain what they were seemingly trying to put behind them. The devastation in the wake of World War II was held up as a mirror to mankind. Here the three people that had concentrated on their own vengeance began to realize that mankind owes itself something different.

Chapter 7

Patrick had merged his airline with his father's trucking firm. This way they could have transport of foods and other goods reduced in cost by eliminating the middleman and charge cheaper prices. The government was trying to have this practice defined as a violation of the Sherman Antitrust Act. This occurred at a time during which Craine, Rodin, and Donny were looking for socially redeeming motives to which they could begin to create a sense of noble ideation and behavior. They were trying to recreate the feeling of camaraderie and brotherhood that the war promoted, but they wanted to expand the notion to apply to the camaraderie of both sides to open the idea of the brotherhood of Man. Part of this thinking was due to the conscience pricking that had begun with the near miss of Tandry's attempt to discredit them. An additional portion of it was the awareness of the next war the world would have, and would leave a devastated pile of sand where people had dwelled. An additional prong that opened up the direction of their efforts was the marriage of Ki followed by a near fatal heart attack. He had always been regarded as part of the group and a unifying aspect of it, due to the violent racist attack that brought him into contact with this bunch of men that believed in the ideals for which they had fought. For his sake a push toward brotherly love was put into motion.

Donny was reminded by his wife that his sons and daughter were reaching awareness of what is right and what is wrong and that they were beginning to understand the principle that a gambling establishment was built on cashing in on Man's weakness: greed. She wanted her children to know their father as a righteous man with principles for them to follow, not to avoid. As ammunition, she used the argument that children of Mafia Dons judged themselves and their fathers as having weak characters and low values of life. He also remembered how Ki's father had died in a position of shame at the hand of the country that was supposed to be standing up for democracy and that this mentor of his was the recipient of hostile feelings that drove him to drugs and a heart that was prone to weakening.

When they all visited Ki they talked about Ira Hayes, Guy Gabaldon, and the Japanese officer that had committed Hara Kari. They talked about how Guadalcanal and Iwo Jima were homes of non-warring peoples that were demolished by the warring powers that could think only in terms of strategies that involved air and tank bases. To what did these people return? The horror of the war had to be shown for all of humanity to say "Never again," as the Jews said it. The thought behind this was that never again would bitterness create haves and have nots that knew only violent and aggressive solutions that had been practiced for centuries. For this reason the UN was created. Along with this body, a reminder had to be erected. Here, at this point, the trio of vengeance seekers decided to direct their efforts. They had reached a point in their thinking that symbolized the knowledge that if we don't begin to care about each other, there won't be an each other to care about. Out of numerous meetings of the big three vigilantes, emerged a plan to use these two islands that were a symbol of turning around the war as a basis for a reason to abolish war by showing that not caring about each other leads to destroying each other. The idea arose to create a museum dedicated to showing what the war had done to both sides at two points where war strategy had replaced humanity.

The resources would be procured by some of the same methodology by which vengeful measures were brought to bear to strike a cord for the remembrance of the former criminal activity. After visiting both islands, they discovered that both peoples wanted to forget about the wreckage of the war. As a result, they came up with the idea of housing the museum in a paddleboat and submarine that toured the battle sites of The Pacific Theater of Operations. Molly, Randi, Penny, LeBere, Becky, and Ms. Doleman all wanted to participate. They were given the tasks of interviewing, coordinating information, deciding on the placement of Memorabilia, and also helping to raise money. This constituted contacts with army, navy, marines, and air force enlisted officers, regular G.I.'s, family members of victims and survivors, Senators, Congressmen, draft boards on both sides, sifting and organizing tons of data as well as businesses in ports of call where leaves were spent. The men and Penny gave deductions in air fare, reduction in fees for truck tonnage, debt reductions for monies owed The Diced Chick. This tactic was already a violation of the Sherman Antitrust Act, in that it encouraged monopolistic practices by granting favoritism to encourage dealing with a company exclusively, due to special treatment, instead of making a choice based on the competitive quality of the services. The technical violation was Suppressing Innovation, as compared with a competitive market. The reduced prices constituted preservation of a monopolistic structure by an illegal tactic.

Unfortunately criminal activity to enable a noble purpose had other forms that were a cooperative activity. Craine had maintained a connection with The Winter Hill Gang. From various members he learned how to fix horse races. He went to the bookie and bought a bloc of tickets. He sold them to some friends in the local teamsters' union at one of their meetings with the proviso that if their horse won, 15% of the winnings went to a fund for building the museum. If this deal was not followed, the offending party would have to deal with the Mullen Gang, an enforcer crew. Craine was able to integrate what he had learned in Ireland and in his days of enforcing the act of unionization with Bugsy Moran. His son's war buddy, Corlando, bought 45 tickets at bets of $1,000. After he paid his 15%, he invested $15,000 in Penny's company. He also placed a bet of $50,000 on a fixed Roulette wheel. The wheel operator was a sister-in-law of Scherlien and communicated with her "sister" regularly. Scherlien, who had left The Diced Chick in bitterness had a man friend in the Senate that was related to Mictal Ornam. Using the wiles available to her, she reawakened the questions begun by Tandry Obrits that were squashed by his deportation.

The local Mafia Dons were offended by the trio for several reasons: 1) The murder of Don Dombrero, 2) the loss of Scherlien

Dotson as an informer to build a blackmail possibility on Donny's drawing money away from their coffers, 3)Craine's dealing with the Irish Winters Mob when the Italian Patriarca family was just as available, 4) Rodin's son getting off the hook, causing one their most professional loan sharks to be killed, 5) The break up and subsequent loss of the Ruozo family as a source for heroin and cocaine. The contract method had failed to bring them under control; perhaps some of their trickery could be employed against them.

Some of the areas of vulnerability would be probed by observing how and where they moved with this museum plan to clean up their names. For instance, Patrick's wife, Randi was pregnant with their first child. Rodin's son, Randal, was attending college on the GI Bill. Penny was doing well in her business, but had to leave her son alone a lot or take him to work with her, which she chose to do. Mictal had endeared himself to Donny and his business, but his support of him made his Senator and Representative relatives suspicious of him. If the Mob were looking for targetable activities, they had plenty to choose from. However, the vacuum created by the absence of Don Dombrero had to be filled.

Section IV

Prisoners and Retaliation

Chapter 1

Scherlien felt as if she were without a vocation since she left The Diced Chick. The loan shark that was harassing Randal for his boss that was killed had ambitions, but he was putty in her hands. She resolved to play up to him so that he would give her more power until she was able to replace him via the route of cement shoes. She saw him as too dumb to catch onto her game. She started out by taking a paralegal course and jockeying herself into the position of Consigliera, so that she could give legal advice, build herself into a powerful position, and observe the power blocs with whom to align herself to gain power. While she did this, she continued her education into law school. Bobby Clippingbird was her teacher in Contract Law. She did not know he was Donny's brother because he used an alias. He informed Donny of this. She flaunted herself at him for a grade, and he played along with it and began to date her. She was making more and more powerful allies and dumped the loan shark off of his own yacht, which she promptly took over in her name. She made a move toward the next Don that had the head of a family rubbed out and took it over. He did this with a couple more families. She began assuming the Consigliera role for the families, secretly built allies by casting suspicions on his sincerity to the families and had some loyal soldiers (to her) take him out into an alley for a good time with a prostitute, who occupied an apartment there. She enticed him into losing his rationality and plunged a knife into his back. There were no more rivals to take over the families into which she had created a leadership vacuum and could easily take over the position of Capo Di Capi. She did not know that Bobby knew about her advances and her ruthlessness and that Donny was planning to retaliate with his own forces.

However, she began to move on her own plan quickly. She had more sense than to hit Donny's family directly because of the way he had nailed her in the past: She did reserve a special corner of her hatred for him because of the embarrassing way he had gotten the confession out of her about where his wife and kids were. The indirect way she chose was to get at Mictal through the Senator and Congressman. She wanted them to be her tools without question; consequently she created an aura of fear and blackmail. Her relative still worked for Donny. She arranged for a fixed game of which pictures were taken of the tilted roulette wheel. Along with this shenanigan, a rendezvous was arranged with a prostitute and videotaped through a camera placed in the ceiling light switch. Thus, the operation to portray Donny as a crooked gambler was begun. She did not realize that sex was so good with Bobby and began to fall in love with him. Of course, this led to her wanting to trust him with her secrets, which went back to Donny. Donny was only one site for vengeance. Another was Randal, the victimized gambler. Donny got word first and relayed the news to Rodin. His partner Craine brought back an old trick to get the pressure off of Randal. In the first place he was to gain proficiency in the use of the .357 magnum and quick skill with a knife. Both weapons were to be licensed, and there was to be sufficient hours of practice to maintain the licensure. Second: Randal was introduced to certain men of the Winter gang, who were bodyguards and on 24 hour call for Randal's needs. He was finished with undergrad school and had been accepted into a medical school program. He had gone to lab to trace the circulation and neural pathways of the nerves to the musculature of the eye on his cadaver. He had his weapons under his lab coat, and two bodyguards were in the lab pretending preoccupation with dissection. Two husky males and a woman came into the lab. They looked too old to be students, although this was getting harder to tell.

Randal nudged the guards, and they got behind the three newcomers in a nonchalant manner. When it appeared that no one was looking, a gun was stuck in Randal's ribs. He reached inside his lab coat to pretend he was reaching for a wallet to satisfy a thief and pulled out a knife and slashed the throat of the assailant. The guards moved behind the other two and garroted them. The next day three new unknown bodies were donated to the anatomy lab. A thank you note was sent to Scherlien along with a beautiful bouquet of orchids, reminiscent of the courtly days of Dinty O'Banion. Not far away, the Winter Gang had wiped out the members of the Patriarca family that had showed up for the festivities. Since no one cared to claim reasons for their presence or who they were, the anatomy department had the addition of several new bodies to add to its lab.

Returning to the Drawing Board, Scherlien decided that children were less wary and more vulnerable. The easiest target was Penny. To take the suspicion off of the obvious ways to kidnap children out of the park, an aging gangster was imported from Ireland, Tandry Obrits. He was prepared for three months before the caper by losing his brogue and fifty pounds of weight. The acid test was his getting a seat on the bench in the park where Mictal, Donny, and sometimes McTavish walked at lunchtime, after work, or Saturday mornings. He was there three days when they were, and no one recognized him. He was ready for the next phase of his project. It required a trip to Boston and then Pittsburgh, back to Boston and a final trip to L.A.

Rodin was weeding his garden on one of his rare weekends off from the trucking company. He liked making his yard clean, similar to the way he once tried to clean the world of French imperialism. He chuckled about this, remembering how full of vengeance he used to be. The mailman brought him a letter stating that there was some important mail waiting for him and his wife at the post office. He went in to tell Liana and found her bound hand and foot with a handkerchief stuffed inside her mouth. A gunman was holding a pistol to her temple. He was wearing a mask in the likeness of Al Capone and motioned with his pistol for him to sit down next to his wife. Another masked figure bound him to her. Rodin could smell unmistakably female cologne or essence of perfume on this figure. The hands that bound him felt soft and cared for; the pair were blindfolded and led to a car whose windows were shaded with blinds. Plugs were put in their ears. Suddenly, the car came to a halt, and strong arms lifted the bound couple. They seemed to go up an incline then down some stairs into a foul smelling basement. They were chained to a wall, and their blindfolds and earplugs were not removed. The next sensation that the terrified couple noticed was a sense of motion. They were not gagged and could talk to each other. The next stop was a fishy smelling harbor. The newly disguised Tandry and his female companion stopped at Boston Harbor. Patrick and Randi were walking in their favorite area in Harvard Yard. Behind two shrub bushes on either side of the walkway appeared two masked gunmen: One wore an Al Capone mask. The other one wore a mask in the disguise of a posterior. There was a distinct aroma of perfume from the one wearing the Al Capone mask. Both were bound, gagged, and muffled before being stuffed into the car with blinds. They were placed in a separate room from the other couple. The next feeling of motion was for a longer (perhaps for three days) period. The stopping place seemed to have a lot of hubbub going on in the form of Hispanic rhythms. Penny was called from school at her job that her son was trying to cross the street at recess to retrieve a lost ball and was hit by a truck, and it was stressed that she come right away. On the playground she was greeted by the same masked hoodlums. Her son, Chris, who was tied, gagged, and blindfolded was there. She was trussed up in a similar fashion and bound to her son. They were put into the car and taken to the harbor and put in a compartment by themselves. That night Scherlien and Tandry celebrated in a local bad restaurant. She did not see Donny and Bobby come in after them and move to the back of the establishment and take a table at the back with a real serious expression on their faces.

Donny and Bobby did not notice Scherlien and Tandry, but they noticed her and a man they did not recognize. Bobby took a picture of the man with his ring camera as they went by. They knew that Scherlien had manipulated herself into the Donhood and, by view of the past kidnapping attempt, they suspected the two new kidnappings, and later, the third to be the work of the mob. In the throes of passion she was very loose tongued about her affairs. She did not disclose her position, as La Dona because of Omerta, but other elements of her thinking got lost in the wake of passion. They decided to play down the serious aspects of their dinner, so as not to attract the attention of the mob involved couple.

Around 2:30 A.M. Bobby received a call in the form of an unrelenting need to celebrate a success in her business relationships with his presence. The voice at the other end said she'd be over in ten minutes because she did not need to wear much. He indicated that the pleasure would be all his. She hung up with a sexy laugh. She opened up her coat the minute she got there to reveal her beautiful nakedness and began to tear at his clothes. She drew him to her and began to kiss him all over and dragged him to his bedroom and sat astride him screaming and moaning. When their lovemaking was over, and they stopped to smoke a cigarette, she told him that certain of her enemies would be making her rich and more powerful in her world of business. They were to be taken to a place outside of the U.S.A., and an exorbitant ransom would be demanded that would weaken her enemies. After all, a woman had to learn how to take care of herself in the rough world of men. Bobby suggested to her that she was very capable of taking care of herself. He turned to her again and she began to moan and demanded that he take her harder and make her scream for more. They reached a point at which they could take no more. Without his asking, she revealed the identities of the captives and stated that she did not know where they would be taken.

Suggestions for a site were being debated at the present time by Tandry and others of the council, who had orders from La Dona to limit the choices to 2 or 3 places. They thought about Eritrea, next to Ethiopia but rejected it because of the tension between the two nations preventing a smooth flow of ransom money; likewise Canada was rejected because of the ties between American police and the Royal Mounties. The final site selected was a small nation in an out of the way place, Andorra, in the Pyrenees Mountains between Spain and France. The country appeared to be peaceful, stable of rebellion, and prospering. Basque agitation for freedom and remnants of this discontent were periodical. During the Spanish Civil War (1936-1939) it seemed to be the site of the imprisonment of the prisoners. Basque agitation was not considered to be a point of major concern. With the other potential sites eliminated, this would be the topic of discussion with La Dona the next day.

At the meeting, all three sites were brought up, and both Ireland

and Sicily were considered and rejected because of the obviousness of the strife, and relationships in the past and the fact that mob connections would be suspected, and the mob was Sicilian in origin. Scherlien's choice was to go along with the choice of Andorra. Arrangements were to be made within three days to get phony passports for the transporters and get a berth on a ship. They also needed to devise a cover for the real reason for the transport of the six prisoners under phony visas. Before shipment could be arranged, the soldiers were instructed to learn as much about the country as they could and to establish a reliable contact that would not get itchy fingers around the exchange of money.

Chapter 2

Andorra is a small country that has remained outside of European history except for its ties to Spain and France. From 1278 until 1993 it had the status of a suzerainty ruled by a Spanish bishop and the king (later the president) of France. During the years of the Spanish Civil War, France was protective of its falling under the control of General Franco. During the war there was much smuggling between Vichy France and Spain that went on. In 1993 a parliamentary form of government was chosen, so that today it is a suzerainty only in name. It enjoys a tourist attraction of winter sports, and is of commercial interest to other nations because of low taxes and lack of customs duties. The principal languages are Catalan, French, Castillian Spanish, and Portuguese. These are also the main groups that make up the population. Into this environment, the six prisoners were cast.

No one knew where they had been taken. They were isolated into separate compartments, but they knew each other by their voices and could establish communication through the walls. The first task that the captives engaged in was to get out of their blindfolds, ear plugs, and gags. They loosened their ropes to allow freedom of movement. They did not know their captors, but suspected Mob connections from the past kidnapping. The main task consisted of developing an escape plan. Since most guards wanted to be liked by their captives, they decided to bring the attention to Chris because no one likes to present his/herself as being cruel to a child.

Penny was the likely candidate to attract male attention because she was single and because she was Chris' mother. She told him to act like he wanted some attention besides hers. Dominic was a robust, egotistical male that could easily be led by a sexy voice and the hint of further things to come. When he was the one the kidnapers chose to

111

feed the captives, she encouraged Chris to act as if he needed the attention of a man by getting hard to manage, being bored, feeling lonely for a male buddy, etc. Dominic began to spend a little time with him playing games, talking about cowboys or sports figures, tussling with him playfully. Now that the stage was set, Penny went into the second act of her ruse. She started playing the helpless woman, showing a little leg, bending towards him with her decolletage partially exposed, turning away from Dominic and bending to show the lines of her posterior; she could see by his behavior, his awkward stammering and aversion of his eyes when she turned to him all of a sudden. This flattered her ego and caused her to chuckle to herself and amongst the other women in their conversations through the walls.

Randi was beginning to show and was having trouble with morning sickness; Since he had become vulnerable to Penny's wiles, she asked Dominic that she be allowed to spend some time with her to help her through the mornings. This time was used to discuss which floor would be most vulnerable to being torn open and covered daily to hide a tunnel and how to let their loved ones know where they were. Patrick's room was chosen because it was closest to the outside trash can, into which dirt could be poured. Rodin knew that all of Craine's trucks were equipped with a fuzzbuster to intercept police messages. He reasoned that once they got out of this house, that a message could be sent via the interpolice. This also meant that Craine could not resort to his usual shenanigans when it came to extricating them from their predicament. Disposing of the dirt from the digging also had to be strategized. Dominic was also suckered in to this. He bought Chris a special lunchbox to make friends with his little buddy. Penny used it to bring medication and proper food for a pregnant woman to Randi. It was used to carry dirt to the nearest receptacle and dumped. Penny was also able to convince Dominic to give the captives some chores to do under supervision of the captors. The chores were a cover for activity related to working on the tunnel. Dominic was so enamored with Chris and Penny that he began to see himself as a father and a suitor to Penny. The next phase was to allow the prisoners to have time together. They planned to devote this time to putting their heads together and to find a way to get their message to Craine and the others on the outside.

During his work during the war, Rodin had contact with several Basques and Catalans that were agitating for freedom from Spain and watched by the French to keep Franco from turning Spain into a fascist state. Information was smuggled out of Andorra to the Free French in England. Rodin recognized the gardener at the house as one of his informants he had used at that time. He was trying to make a contact with this person, who knew what he was about and realized that his employer was connected to the Mob. Hence, he rebuffed any attention that Rodin threw his way. He knew that this man, Raoul, was very vulnerable to women, not the way Dominic was, but in a more adventurous way, sort of like the man of song that was attracted to older women. He and Liana recalled some of their adventures at teasing Germans and other adversaries in Canada, New York, and the orient and decided to construct a scheme to pull Raoul out of his fearful security. Raoul was attracted to Liana during his alliance with Rodin and was very fearful of seeking involvement with her because he had heard what had happened to anyone that crossed him when he wanted something. He was in the bar the day Rodin stuck a knife in the German's neck. Liana began a flirtation with Raoul, according to a plan with her husband. She acted interested in the Basque and invited him to a rendevous, which was interrupted by Rodin coming home from his doing chores. He held a carving knife at Raoul's throat that brought back the memory of the last event involving a throat and a knife He asked the gardener if he could think of a reason why Raoul shouldn't enjoy the same fate as the German. The Basque stammered that he would help him in his present skirmish with the Mafia. Rodin said that he would honor this request, as long as Raoul would be of help to the prisoners. This loyalty would wipe the slate clean.

Now that agreement to take the risk was decided upon, the tasks were defined. The first step in repayment for the life saved was that this employee of the household had to procure weapons for the prisoners, which were a tommy gun and pistol for each prisoner with several rounds of bullets, knives for each, dynamite with lengthy fuse attachments, a cannon and cannonballs to be hidden underground until needed. He also was to arrange for false passports so that exit from the country without being detected by the Mob was possible. The last task was to inform Craine via the fuzzbuster where they were and to arrange the secret transport of any available help to their site to aid the escape. A meeting date was also to be arranged, along with a deadline to have their tunneling out plans completed. Raoul also understood that treachery or informing of their captors would mean a burial next to the German. It was also made known that if Rodin did not carry out the execution, one of the prisoners or their compadres would.

The cannon and cannonballs were strategically placed in a cave on the mountain as near as could be placed and still destroy their prison that had been dug to store munitions during the war. Its geography was such that the house was at the center of the trajectory arc of the cannon. The message was received by Craine. He informed the others and started to get them planning their readiness for the mob warfare he had once before experienced with the plane. The Winters Mob was consulted; they developed a twofold strategy: Keep the mob occupied with a war by infringing on the Mob's territory and forcing them to use part of their manpower by going to the mattresses with them and training Craine, Mictal, Randal, Bobby and Donny in smoking out the captors, and training LeBere, Molly, and Scherlien's sister-in-law who had been working as a double agent in Donny's gambling establishment, spying on La Dona while she was working there while pretending to work with her, and Becky in the ways to use their feminine sides to glean information from people that they suspected had it to give. Needless the plane would be crowded with reinforcements. They estimated that they would be ready to roll in about three weeks.

Scherlien wanted her victims under her control. She composed a ransom note and sent it to Donny, who in turn sent it to Craine. The content of the note stated: This group of enemies of theirs owed them $60,000 in reparations for dealing with an Irish gang on Italian turf, $150,000 for ransom of the six captives, and $120,000 as reparations for the death of Don Dombrero. She knew that even the wealthy Donny would have difficulty raising this amount of money. They were supposed to meet at La Dona's summer home on Cape Cod with the money, and the prisoners would be released.

Craine responded with a triumvirate action: He fitted the plane with four extra machine guns, several rockets, and harpoon guns with explosives attached to the end of the harpoons. He then got hold of Raoul via his fuzzbuster and told Rodin and Patrick to be ready to do battle with their captors in two weeks The last task was to meet the representative of the Mob on Cape Cod. Instead of paying him off, they forced him into a car and blindfolded him. They drove him past the docks and conversed about getting cement for the shoes. The gangland soldier could tell by the fishy smell that he was at the pier; he began to sweat through the blindfold. Next they took him to a forested area known to be inhabited by wolves. They took his blindfold off so that he'd know where he was then put it back on. They took his shirt off and put a combination of hamburger meat and honey all over his chest and handcuffed him to a tree. They left him there for three hours and returned to find him dead. They took off his trousers, flew over the Cape Cod house and parachuted the feces filled pants onto the roof then flew away. The Diced Chick ship was loaded with cannons and machine guns and dispatched to Lisbon Harbor where armed men would disembark and head for the Pyrenees, and the boat would await any escapees from the Mob trying to flee.

Having not yet heard about the reversal that had occurred, Scherlien wanted to celebrate; she gave Bobby a call and invited him to a homemade Italian dinner. He agreed to bring a bottle of Lambrusco wine. His actual intent was to put arsenic in the wine and eliminate a vicious killer. The dinner looked scrumptious: veal parmesan with a creamy mushroom sauce, a side dish of linguini with stuffed meatballs, cooked in the same Lambrusco wine that Bobby had brought, a bowl of Italian Wedding Soup, and Caolis with spumoni on top. Before the wine, La Dona took him by the hand to the living room, sat him on the couch, and put a CD of *Lara's Theme* on the machine. As the voice began to make itself heard, she pulled him to dance with her. She curled her arms about his neck, and he could feel her nipples hardening against his chest. She began to unbutton his shirt and to play with her fingers in the hairy chest beneath her hands. She began to reach for him and could feel him growing in her hand. Quickly, he undid her blouse and freed her breasts from the cumbersome brassiere she wore. He kissed and touched them tenderly and marveled over how beautiful they were. Scherlien pulled him down on the couch and reached inside his trousers and stripped the garments off of him, stroking him all the while. He reached the back of her skirt and unzipped it and felt beneath her thong, gently tugging it off of her. He caressed her bottom slowly and began to kiss her thighs, murmuring how smooth and powerful they felt. He then began to nuzzle her triangle, and she began to open herself to him and to moan at a high pitched sound that grew in intensity. Suddenly she grasped him and put him inside her. They both began to rock, and the room appeared to shake. They reached their peak and lay for a half hour nuzzling each other. At this point, Bobby said that some wine would be nice, and he got up to go to the kitchen and poured. He had found the vial of arsenic in his discarded pants and found himself unable to pour it into the wineglass and poured it down the drain.

Chapter 3

Having brought the wine in to La Dona and placing the glass before her, she took it from him and cooed at the first sip. She got a phone call at that point, and he saw her expression change from one of contentment to one of rage. He heard her say hotly what did you do with the damn pants. He heard a gruff voice say, "They're in the Atlantic."

"What are we supposed to do with them?" he heard the official voice of La Dona speak into the receiver. "Start questioning the prisoners and apply torture, but don't kill anyone .They're worth more to us alive than dead. Obviously, we'll get more information if we start with the kid. Next hit the pregnant woman, and do it in front of her husband."

A chill went through Bobby as he heard this, but he was more surprised when she began to stroke his face to resume their previous level of activity. He was able to make himself respond as previously, but the enthusiasm was no longer there. He thought to himself that had he seen this, he would have been able to pour the arsenic into the glass.

As soon as Bobby thought Scherlien was asleep, he phoned Donny, who in turn phoned Craine. Craine got on the fuzzbuster and reached Patrick. He relayed Scherlien's message and told him to get everyone out of there. He also got directions to the cave and advised them that he was immediately sending The Diced Chick ship to Lisbon Harbor with the promised reinforcements and weapons. He also armed the plane with rockets, extra machine guns, and harpoons and harpoon guns with dynamite attached. He said he'd be down with the plane in a few days.

A sound was heard outside the door. Rodin reached for his gun and pulled the door open. Raoul was seen listening there; the Basque backed off and raised his hands, then turned and ran. Rodin took aim and fired, splattering Raoul on the floor. Dominic was preparing supper for Penny and Chris when he heard the sound. He dropped the tray, pulled his gun, and ran for Penny's room. He pulled the door open and was sprawled out on the floor by Chris knocking his legs out from under him with the ball bat Dominic had bought for him. Penny scooted over to the gun and picked it up, pointing it at Dominic. He raised his hands and pleaded, "You've got me wrong. I want to help. God help me, Penny, I was going to tell you this tonight. I've fallen in love with you. I want to help get you out of here." Penny took this news skeptically. Rodin and Patrick opened the door suddenly and said they needed all the manpower they could get. They warned Dominic that he would be summarily shot if any suspicious behavior would occur.

There were seven guards posted as guards and twenty-six more people throughout the house. Two men were on the roof, two at the front door, and two at the back, one in the basement. Dominic went down the basement stairs and stabbed the guard in his chest. At the same time, Randi faked a bleeding episode, and the two guards at the front door rushed to her. She hit one in the throat with a heavy pipe, smashing his Adam's apple and choking him, put the pipe on the gun, and silently shot the other one. She ran around to the back door and shot the guard, who was about to shoot Chris for knocking the other one down with his bat. Before he could get up, she fired and hit him in the head. The only two left were the ones on the roof. Patrick climbed on the back roof and Rod in the front. Each pushed his man down. When they landed, Penny shot the one in front and threw her gun to Liana. Liana ran around to the back and shot the other one.

Dominic asked one of the others for the keys to the jeep to get some bread. After he tossed him the keys, Dominic stabbed him in the throat and ran for the jeep, pulling in front of the house and signaled the escapees to get in. They were freed, but they did not know where they were going.

To avoid easy detection and being easy targets, they decided to mingle with the French and Spanish tourists in the old quarter of the city in which they were turned loose, Andorra la Vella. The streets were narrow in this quarter. They had access to the public square from this spot. Here locals mingled with the tourists. Through a priest at the Cathedral, they were able to locate two reliable guides to take them to the mountains close to where their cave with the weapons in it could be found. They could converse in French and Spanish sufficiently enough to be understood and to understand what was being said about them. Penny heard the tail end of a conversation between the guides about her breasts and thighs. With a slight giggle, she bent over seductively, giving them both an eyeful then stepped on one's foot with her high heel and dug it in his shoe toe.

Dominic didn't like the way the conversation was going and moved over to Penny in a protective manner with a serious look on his face. The guides didn't want any trouble and moved away from the confrontation. They took them to the mountains and left in as hasty a way as they could. The escapees did not have any trouble finding the cave, and located their comfort zones then gathered wood for a fire to warm themselves and to cook the food they had stolen from the house. Dominic was self conscious and stood off to the side by himself in a corner. Penny and Chris sidled over to him. Chris hugged him for protecting his mother. Penny stroked back the bangs of hair that hung in his face and took his hand. Suddenly she kissed him very gently and stroked his face again. She laughed and said, "I sort of like big bad gangsters that are gentlemen underneath all that macho bravado." He sheepishly grinned at her and related that there was a lot in his life that provoked him to anger, but he didn't like himself for that anger. He also relayed that he had done a lot of ugly things and was not particularly proud of himself for them.

Chapter 4

Back in Boston and Virginia Craine was rounding up the Winters gang and his family, along with whatever conglomeration of weapons, bombs, bullet proof vests, and ammunition he could muster. Molly wanted to join him, but he put his foot down so she stayed at home. He had directions to the cave. He instructed the group to find a cave that was close to a butte with shrubs around it so that he could land the plane and could mount the guns in the bushes and not be seen without difficulty. He also maintained radio contact with the ship and ordered the captain to look for a river that led from the harbor to the mountains. Such a river could not be found on the Portuguese coast. Consulting an atlas, the shipmaster located the Ebro River, which emptied into a delta on the East coast of Spain at Tortosa and turned north to join the Segre River, which flowed into Andorra to Andorra Vella, and to the mountains. It would take The Diced Chick about two days to sail around Spain to get there. Craine gave orders that the floating casino needed to begin its trip immediately. It was off and running. Boar's Tusk knew his business when it came to planning a journey to do battle with the white aggressor. He had waited with patient, smoldering rage for this day.

The boat pulled into a cove that was covered with shrubs to hide it. More branches and greenery were added to the camouflage. When the plane landed on the butte nearby, it was similarly hidden from view. The first matter at hand was to find out how much progress was made on the tunnel. It was a good deal past the house and between a third and halfway to the mountains completed. A decision had to be made whether to extend it further or to use it as far as it was dug. If the former, they were risking allowing the enemy access to their fortress by allowing them to be able to tunnel through to where the cave was;

if the latter, then a door would have to be erected and locked from the cave side. On the other side, the ground could be mined with explosives to prevent escape of the Mafiosos from an invasion of the house. The decision that was made was to lock the house off and mine the ground on the house side of the door. This began late that night.

The door was taken in a wagon to the furthest advance of the tunnel, and the debris was pushed aside to allow access; after laying the mines in place and locking the other side of the door, the debris was replaced with cement, covered with artificial turf to conceal it. The next move was to develop a line of motile weaponry. With monies from Donny's coffers, four sailboats had been bought and fitted for mountain terrain wheels. The next move was to cart them to the mountains. Then they were fitted for cannons at each end, as well as harpoon guns.

Word had finally gotten back to Scherlien, and she ordered her men to the mattresses against the rescuers, which included the Winters gang; with them already there was a state of gang warfare going on. The guides were located, and under pressure, they disclosed all that they knew about where they had taken the escaped prisoners. Unfortunately for them, the cave was camouflaged, as were the weapons. The guides were to take the gangsters as far as they had gone with the escapees. Since they did not know the site of the cave, they began burning to smoke out the runaways. There was no response, and the cave and weaponry were not detected. The weapons were not even there.

They were not there because they had launched an attack on the house and were moving toward their target. Rodin was the first to notice that no one was there. He saw what looked like a couple of corpses and moved closer, finding the bodies of the two guides. Figuring out what had happened was not too hard. They decided to wait in a hidden portion of the property and await the return of the gangsters. One third of them went into the house through the tunnel and locked the door on the outside. The rest were manning the converted sailboats. Craine had his plane in the bushes ready for a swoop at the mobsters and their house of ransom.

About five cars pulled up in front of the house. The boats began firing and moved up on them. The gangsters got behind the cars and began firing back. The faction from in the house moved to the door and commenced their shooting. One of them had a howitzer and fired it in the middle of the circle of cars, blasting a hole in the circle and allowing the prisoners' gunmen to burst through. Penny and Dominic had remained at the cave and were shelling the house and firing harpoons with dynamite and flaming rags attached at the fortress. A few gangsters sneaked in the back door with Tommy guns and made their way to the roof. They were firing at the prisoners that had made their way to the circle of cars. Rodin was hit. Craine had been warming up the plane. He fired at the roof while the plane was taxiing and yelled for someone to get Rodin out of there. Patrick ran over to him and saw blood gushing from his leg. He ran to the nearest car, and it had a driver in it, shooting at him. Patrick jumped onto the hood and shot him through the window. With a move quick as lightning, he jerked the door open, climbed in, and hit the brake with his foot. He then ran out to Rodin and lifted him into the car. Rodin tore his shirt off and applied a tourniquet to his blood spurting leg. Pat lay down, warning him to keep his pistol handy, but to stay out of the gunfight. By this time, Craine was already in the air and began strafing the gangsters. One of them turned around and began shooting at the plane with his tommy gun. Craine fired a rocket at him and blew him into about 50 pieces. He then climbed the plane and dropped a bomb on the roof. That ended the battle. The remaining gangsters surrendered and were securely tied to a tree with a fire around it to keep off wolves. Hamburger meat was put at spots in the periphery of the fire to attract the beasts. The police were called, the weapons were gathered from the cave and elsewhere, the prisoners got into the sailboats with wheels and went to The Diced Chick, then home. Rodin was taken to a doctor. Chris went home with his Uncle Pat and Aunt Randi, while his mother and Dominic remained behind and would catch up with the others in a week.

Chapter 5

Scherlien was in a fury. She could not understand how 6 untrained captives could withstand the incarceration by over 20 trained soldiers and escape from them and cause at least 15 of them to join their Mob in the sky. She learned about the close relationship between Bobby and Donny through Tandry and she realized that she had herself to blame for her fallibility. She also did not like losing the fancy house she had bought in Andorra to the damage of a bomb and rocket or having the roof of her Cape Cod house stunk up by a pair of dirty pants. She met with Tandry to devise a plan to eliminate both Donny and Bobby at the same time.

The plan they devised involved her acting as if nothing had happened and invite Bobby for more of the same as he had the last time. Scherlien would let information leak to Donny that she was holding him for ransom, and when he tried to rescue his brother, Tandry would be waiting for him.

Bobby knew what she had up her sleeve, and he brought back the arsenic to beat her at her own game. He seduced her and let her seduce him in the same way as they had done the last time. He still had difficulty pouring the arsenic into her drink. She had concealed a gun with a silencer on it beneath her pillow. She was looking for an appropriate break in the lovemaking to reach for the pistol, but it was so tense and felt so good that she could not stop. When he got up to get the drinks, he finally poured the poison into hers and returned to her. She was lying there naked pointing a pistol at him. She told him his love was beautiful, but she knew that Donny was his brother and knew how he had thwarted her schemes. She hated what she had to do because she'd never had a lover like him and probably never would again. He saw her hand shake with the gun in it, and was able to pull it out of her hand. He threw it on the floor and said that they should resume where they had left off. She smiled and drew him to her. They touched and kissed teasingly and seekingly and finally with demand and power unleashed that could control a universe. They lay snuggled with each other, and Scherlien reached for her drink. Reflexively, Bobby knocked it out of her hand and said, "It's poisoned, don't. I guess I feel the same way you do. What'll we do about it?" She touched him gently and sensuously and said she didn't know.

On the roof, Tandry was crouched behind the chimney awaiting his victim. Donny appeared and looked around to make sure no one was within eyesight and knelt down so that he wouldn't be seen. Tandry crept up behind him with his knife ready for his victim's throat. "Ah, me boyo; ye're not as smart as ye thought." (The excitement of a kill brought back the brogue.) "Oh no," he chortled and threw his body into his assailant's and whirled around to face him, the way his wrestling coach had taught him. Tandry saw that he also had a knife in his hand. He slashed at Donny only to turn backward as a harpoon behind him pierced his left shoulder blade and his heart. The last vision he had was that of McTavish Mikawber getting up from the roof behind him with a harpoon gun in his hand.

The issue between Scherlien and Bobby had to be resolved. They were too attached to each other to let go, yet they could not maintain a relationship with one on one side of the law and one on the other side. Bobby was not about to give up a respected position as an attorney to become a tool of the rackets. Therefore, Scherlien had to choose whether or not she wanted to maintain her position of power or be loved. Scherlien remained enrolled as Bobby's law student, and this factor had to be disposed of or pursued in the wake of a difficult decision. She chose to remain in Andorra on a temporary leave of absence from school while she made up her mind. This also entailed her finding loyal body guards outside of the Mob.

Not all of the rain that falls in our lives is controlled by how we respond to it. Death is inevitable, and it now came into the lives of our group and took its toll on our fiends' souls. Dorlando had bought himself time with a transplant, but human tissue does not last forever, and the piper had to be paid. He was grocery shopping with LeBere and slumped over a shopping cart. She went on talking to him until she discovered that he didn't answer and looked in his direction. She let out a loud scream for help and began to administer CPR; it was too late. When he got to the hospital, he was DOA. With a tremor in her hands and in her voice, she called her sons. With this same shaking, she attempted to drive home and skidded into a tree, snapping her neck. At least they would spend eternity together.

Donny, Bobby, Rodin, Patrick, and Ki each presented a part of the eulogy: first Rodin spoke about the heroism with which he and Patrick came to him to help wipe out the menace of Nazi-ism and how the need to find love in all this ugliness drove him to watch LeBere and to pull away from the destruction of war he had come to perpetrate. Ki related that this couple had done what they could to wage the peace by practicing forgiveness to the former enemy and passing such thinking on to their sons. He testified to the generous spirit that tore a bully off of him and helping him build a life of recovery based on mutual forgiveness. He added that his life would not be the same since he could no longer bask in LeBere's and Dorlando's sea of brotherhood. Donny and Bobby spoke together about how the brotherhood and courage to believe in the basic love of human beings for one another led their parents to reach across the ugliness that was the reservation to bring them into a world in which there was something to build on, other than hatred. They both stated that they would never forget the parents that taught them to survive in other than a cesspool. Donny thanked them for teaching him to value the love of his wife and kids above the striving and to see this as his haven from the constant battle for vengeance. In reality, he was not sure that he was ready to give up his resurrection of Tecumseh's dream.

Bobby, on the other hand, later reflected on the fact that he was able to forgive Scherlien her violent ways to find the possibility of love. He thought of it as a possibility because she had to choose between the path she had taken and a relationship with him. As is the usual outcome of a grieving process, those left behind to live had to undergo the building of strength to live without the guidance of the deceased to cope with what stresses lay ahead of them. In other words, the memory of their lost one had to be integrated with what their own lives had taught them.

The internal debate was not just confined to those who gave the eulogy, but manifested itself amongst the entire group. The struggle to create something that all humanity would share that was laid aside was about to be reawakened in their minds and in their actions. The building of the museums to stand as a symbol of the horror of a bloody war was about to be resumed. Patrick put the cap on this when he recalled the speech in 1930 when he was declared a man by Jewish tradition. He brought up the topic how Dorlando went beyond the dollar chasing, about which the young Pat had spoken that day; how he believed in the spirit of Man when he went back to a blown up munitions plant to let his future wife know that she was for him, his horror at having to face the guns of kids at Remagen, how he had invested the wealth he had accumulated to pull two worthy boys out of a demeaning reservation life, and how much Dorlando and LeBere ignored material advantage to pass out love to those they knew. He concluded that the remaining work in their legacy to those that followed or stood with them in their path lay in delineating the horror of the war that was the logical consequence of greed and dollar chasing.

Craine and Rodin added that they all had contributed to the violence that stemmed from the greed and materialism they learned as kids, even though it was administered as a protective measure. They urged their friends and families to give them the chance to strive to bring out the gentle and loving part of the nature of Man because their time was short.

Section V

Waging the Peace

Cry Heaven, Cry Hell

Chapter 1

Waging peace is a lot harder than waging war. In war we are trained to unleash the anger we have in us because we are asked to put our life on the line for someone we don't know and to disrupt our plans at someone else's bidding. To wage peace we have to accept someone else's kind and/or noble gesture, regardless of whether or not they brought destruction and violence to our country or not, whether or not the peace is waged with sincerity and good intentions or to show a sense of feeling morally superior to a vanquished enemy. The group trying to start the museums had to deal with all these feelings plus rehashing the memories of buddies or close relatives slain and gone from the lives of the survivors behind them.

One of the hardest hit was Ki. He had to go back to the memories of keeping his promise to his father in altering the face of racial prejudice and assignment of blame for the war, as well as reliving the sight of a Hara Kari that drove him to drugs. There also was no more Dorlando to provide support or rescue from the bigots he had encountered and would encounter again. He had to maintain almost constant contact with his sponsor to maintain his sanity. It was with a great deal of effort and the reawakening of a lot of pain that he made the trip to Kobe, Japan and sought out the relatives of the officer that had disemboweled himself before his eyes. He even received the weapon with trembling hands, as he thanked the family for contributing to Man not leading himself/herself to war.

He could not visit the Pima Reservation by himself. Becky and Penny went with him. This was the first time Penny saw the conditions under which Native Americans had to live to preserve their nationality. The family of Ira Hayes was happy to receive and to provide them with mementos of his life. They also remembered that the Pimas were left without help in getting better irrigation techniques or help in their farming methods and continued to starve after Ira Hayes' heroism, and that the country thought it was more important to sell war bonds than to help his tribe find a better quality of life. Ki was especially disturbed by the hypocrisy driving Ira to drink. Becky and Penny had to spend the night in his room with him to keep him from going out and getting drugs.

Because of the powerful effect on Ki, Donny went to visit General Kurabashi's family. They talked about the cost of giving up Bushido to the Japanese and the sublimation that drove Japanese industrialists and businessmen to work themselves at inhuman levels to find a substitute for it. They also mentioned the inhumanity of dropping the atom bomb and how the demanding work ethic was also a sublimation of the rage the Japanese felt toward the Americans, as well as a way to beat them at their own game by taking away their economic supremacy. These former enemies gave the memories of their general in the hope of teaching that hatred of men for each other comes in the wake of scarring wars and the healing needs to be addressed once the war is ended or even before. They also acknowledged that maintaining a war because of clinging to an outmoded code of life was a gross error in judgment that Gen. Kurabashi and many others had made. Hopefully, this museum would help all men look at questioning their codes.

Donny and Becky had to go to the south part of Chicago to interview the family of a black youth, who was killed at Guadalcanal. He was a 2nd lieutenant that had to take over a battalion because the captain that led the charge when the 12,000 Americans hit the beachhead was blown to pieces by machine gunfire, leaving him the next in command. The captain and the young Louie had become fast friends and had agreed to give their girlfriends green pearls they had purchased from an Okinawan peddler when on leave together at Pearl Harbor. If anything happened to one of them, the survivor was to deliver it to the victim's girlfriend. The pearls were identical except for having each one's name carved into it. The Louie's name was Caesar Valparaiso. He had survived the onslaught at Guadalcanal and had sent both pearls to his younger brother to either save for him or send to both girls if anything happened to him. He served at Saipan in the same company as Guy Gabaldon, who taught him Japanese to help urge the enemy soldiers to surrender. He was shot by a soldier emerging from a cave because he had learned to fear Blacks from American he had met before the war. The girls had become friends and kept their pearls, as treasures. However, they each had copies made and gave them to the memory seekers, along with a picture of the grave sites next to each other in Arlington Cemetery. After brushing away his tears, Donny saw his wife crying; to cheer her up he told her a George Jessel joke about a light complexioned black man who was asked what race he was and answered "Human". She smiled and socked him in the shoulder. He also smiled and thought that his father would have given such a response.

Bobby had to go to New York to visit a Mafioso family to get the brass knuckles of a soldier who had enlisted as a marine and got killed while trying to take a machine gun nest on the lower part of Mt. Suribachi. A gyrene next to him asked him to pick out a tooth for him of the first Jap he killed. He turned to him and said, "Nah, pick your nose instead." As he turned to speak, he was shot in the face. He called Scherlien and invited her to go with him. She accepted with a little chilliness from Donny. But he and the others saw another side of her

The museum looked as if it were taking off. The ships seemed to need a stay at home manager. Rodin felt he had a good thing going with his partnership with Craine and Patrick in the merged trucking company and airline. But father and son had charted the direction they had wanted their company to go; even though his deep friendship for the two of them would never let him get out of the company, he began to feel restless and wanted to add something of his own to the life he and Liana were leading. His son, Randal, was in the process of completing medical school and had married the girlfriend he had back in the dreary days of his gambling problem. Their family was well grounded and stable. There was no demand to be an intervening father. He and Liana missed the days of going from nation to nation and berating the French empire. They needed something that was going somewhere for them. Stories of what Ki, Donny, and Bobby had experienced brought a spark of interest and reawakening of the drive to hear stories and situations and plug them into the fixed agenda of promoting some of the brotherhood that Man needed to progress and survive for the world to see began to intrigue them. When Rodin presented his idea to Craine and Patrick, they were happy for the avenue he had found for himself and welcomed his decision to maintain a minimal connection with their partnership and to develop his own area of interest.

He came home and caressed his wife in a way he hadn't done in years and said, "Well, old girl, we're about to be traipsing around the world again. Only now we'll be hustling world peace instead of calling the French names." Liana kissed him and told him how wonderful that was. He wanted to go to bed on that note. She asked him if a certain old goat, who was trying to go back to being a kid again, needed a cold shower instead. He said not unless a certain old bird joined him, which she did.

The first adventure started with an Australian, now living in Montreal that had been trapped in the forced march to Corregidor from Bataan. He had encountered a Japanese officer that treated him extremely cruelly. Not only did he refuse him food and water on the march but he had the temerity to eat a sausage sandwich and drink a cup of Philippine beer in front of his hungry and thirsty victim. The officer noticed a turquoise stone enclosed in a golden case, which the prisoner wore on a golden chain around his neck. He asked him where he got the locket, and the Aussie told him that his mother was killed in a car crash and gave it to him just before she died. Seeing it as being a source of some value at a pawn shop, he snatched it from the prisoner's neck. The man's name was Ollie Dandorf, and his assailant was Imperial Officer Besam Ohira. They would meet again.

The Japanese were occupying Guadalcanal, and the Americans came to wrest it from them to help MacArthur keep his vow to return to the Philippines and because it was part of the strategic Solomons chain, close enough to Japan to be able to launch air attacks. A battalion of Aussies joined the American Marines to help bolster their troop strength. Among these was Staff Sgt. Ollie Dandorf. To avoid the effects of the massive American bombings, the Japanese hid in caves. Ollie and his company had to smoke out the enemy that had a machine gun nest in a cave that was holed up in a cave and impeding the allied advance. Circling around a cliff, they entered the cave from the back and caught the machine gunners from behind and wiped them out. Upon inspection of their damage, Ollie saw some movement. Drawing his automatic, he approached the body he thought he saw movement in, and saw a man lying on the ground with a severely bleeding leg wound. He tore off his shirt and used it as a tourniquet and helped the man to his feet and called for a medic, who took the man to get help. He thought there was something familiar about the Jap, but he dismissed his impression as not important. A week later, he received a call for mail. There was a package with a note inside it. He opened the package and found the locket his mother gave him with a one word note that said "Thanks." The two of them briefly corresponded after the war and drifted apart, but Ollie always kept the note, of which he gave a copy to Rodin. He also gave him a copy of the locket and chain.

Chapter 2

The couple that had terrorized the French empire for years had a change of heart. They called together all the donors and donor chasers together and made plans about what role the museums would have and how to fulfill those roles. The wars left dead in their wakes and hatred as a legacy. The thousands of dead at Ypre bore into the memories of Craine and Rodin. Dorlando took the picture of shooting kids to his grave with him. Ki realized that the picture of the suicide and its associations had to cause him to exercise strong discipline, or he'd find himself the way his friends found him outside that bar. The way to help the victims of the hate/kill syndrome was to provide symbols of the love that exists between human beings where hatred is taught and means survival. Rewards were given for seeking as well as providing exhibits. Seasonal discount passes were available for donors, donor seekers, financial donors, etc. When involved participants wanted the museum ships in the nearest harbor for family or social occasions, such preferences were honored. Tax breaks were given for financial donors, and these included monies willed to the museums.

Hatred is a deeply ingrained feeling and goes to great lengths to create frustrations, and they are clung to with great strength. For example, Bushido, the code of the warrior not only drove the Japanese to justify approaching other cultures with arrogance, but it caused the soldiers to hide in caves, to resist the attempts by an enemy superior in numbers and weaponry to bring about an end to the death trap, called World War II. It forced them to move to a devastating solution that generated further smoldering hatred. The Japanese industrialists, scientists, businessmen all hated the Americans that dropped the bomb that had destroyed much of their lives. They were as willing to beat them at their own game of industrial supremacy and took on the heart conditions, ulcers, and cancers that had plagued the Western powers. Communism grew out of the hatred of the exploitation, and the hatred was escalated by atrocities attributed to either side. Religion was seen as an opiate of the people because it only looked at the rosy eternity it held up to man. The same diversion from hatred could be taught by creating the memory of beauty that existed along with the ugliness. This was the purpose that the La Mondes had in mind.

They would share their change in perceptions with Craine and Molly, Patrick and Randi, Donny and Becky at their social evenings together. The alteration in their views was beginning to get infectious. Scherlien was beginning to be perceived as someone that could receive love for her generous moments, and the kidnappings lost some of the horror to them, as she began to ferret out Mafiosos that had helped allies escape during the war or aid in smuggling Jews out of countries, use Mob money to relieve some of the harshness of ghetto life, or guide would be angry warriors out of the reservations, and have corrupt Indian agents forcibly removed their offices.

Another area where hatred was to erode into a more wholesome feeling was in the disparity in getting out of the financial trap into which one is born or grows up. In this arena, Donny and Bobby and Scherlien took leading roles. They went into war torn zones and used money to create legitimate jobs and provided training in the areas into which they had moved. Their work was done in Barrios and black and white ghettos in America, as well as abroad. Education was also altered. It became a two way street. The educators had to acknowledge that they also had something to learn from the "peasants" they were teaching. This came to the fore in the neighborly discussions at the card playing parties, looking at movies, dinners, etc.

Rodin and Craine had been wanting to see what had changed in Ireland, the training site at Lafayette Escadrille, and the universities in Ontario and Quebec where Rodin and Liana had done their agitation. They had also planned on a return trip to Vietnam to see what needed to be done to assuage the hatred that ensued from the war.

The Greens versus the Oranges got mixed up with nationalistic and religious concerns over the years, and the feelings behind them began to be articulated by terroristic raids on British and Protestant entities by the IRA, which was a reconstituted form of the old Sinn Fein that Craine and his family had learned to love and fight so dearly. The Oranges did not let themselves sit back and be violated. They formed their own organization and gave the Auld Greens as good as they got. The violence between them seemed to drive the Prots to move more toward England politically, and it was exported to other countries, mainly the U.S.A which has a large Irish population. Prison sentences and executions grew in the British Isles, as did prisoners' retaliations via starvation diets, etc. The fact that the Irish had elevated themselves to part of the affluent majority, who were becoming sensitized to their ethnic origins by the emergence of nationalistic awareness of suppressed minorities that began to stand up for themselves, as Ghandi and Martin Luther King Jr. showed them how, money began to be diverted to helping wanted perpetrators of violence escape their fates; monies began to be diverted to assisting "Our brothers in Eire or Erin" in their fight for independence. Not only Irishmen, but Italians, Germans, and Jews joined the disenchanted Blacks and Hispanics in their fights for a piece of the action. This resurgence of nationalism and identity striving had multiple sources of origin.

First and foremost was the desire to be loved by an oppressor. A sense of guilt for punishing those that share our human identity causes prison guards to adopt many of the standards that residents of our penal institutions have because fear of hatred and retaliation for a wrong done pervades their thought. Along with this the adage of do unto others as you want them to do unto you enters the picture.

A second consideration that enters this picture is guilt for making a choice between self and leaving others behind to bear the pain of rejection and being left out of the large circle of affluence available to those that abandon the huddled masses. Entering into this configuration is the idea of missing the warmth between those who suffer together. A good example of this is the missing of the bonds of youth that ties brothers together that are raised by a tyrant, when they separate to find their own lives in adulthood.

Craine and Rodin wandered the streets of Belfast and came upon two gangs of youngsters hurling rocks, broken beer bottles, and other self-made forms of weaponry from the streets at each other. They were behind barricades on opposite sides of the road. A leader on one side saw a way to bring victory to his side by leading a charge at one corner with several boys near him. He encouraged a boy at the other end to do the same at his end at the same time. Anticipating what would happen, Craine nudged Rodin to get involved between the boys at one end while he did so at the other end. What happened was that before the two mini armies became engaged, Craine and Rodin fired shots in the air to startle the gang members on both sides into cessation of hostilities.

The boys were afraid of the guns, but one of them had to come forward and ask these two strange old men what they wanted with them. Craine laid his gun next to him and started to tell them that he grew up on these streets a long time ago and had to leave this land he had known as home because he had learned that you had to fight someone that believed differently than you and, sometimes, had to kill someone because his/her view of right did not agree with yours. He related that the world was at war when he had left. He further pointed out that his friend and he shared the same difference that these boys did. He recalled how the two of them had saved his wife from an enemy or about the field full of dead bodies at Ypre that had occurred because neither side could stand to have his adversary control a few miles of earth. The earth that was left was not fit to grow crops or to build homes on because of the wreckage, the memories of those who were maimed and lost, and the memories of those who were left to remember the destruction of what had once been. Another of the boys piped up with, "What are you tellin' us that's new, Old Geezer. We know all that. It's these Prots that are sellin' our souls to the British devils."

This remark caused the hubbub to begin again, and one of the boys reached for a rock until he felt Rodin's knife at his wrist. The Frenchman continued where Craine had left off. "My family carried a grudge against France for centuries over a piece of land and an injustice. All the people that suffered this injustice are dead, and the land is now a park. The lesson that France had to learn was never taught because she approached others, who were different with the idea that she was superior and righteous and only had something to teach, not to learn from underlings. This is the same thought pattern that my friend and I have just encountered. If you want to be a field of bodies, killed for no reason, other than to stop the other side from having a foothold there, who will have the land? There is some right and wrong in each of us, and we can work out our differences or destroy each other." Craine remembered his being physically attacked for what he believed and that his wife was slain because she believed differently than others. Had the Ornams and he listened to his Da, bloodshed and criminality could have been avoided in his life. Hopefully, these youngsters would learn that they did not have to pollute their lives with hate.

Craine noticed a boy start to grimace. Suddenly he began to charge him with a knife drawn, simultaneously as another headed toward Rodin with a huge rock. Both men were veteran fighters and assumed the most relaxed stance that would provide protection, yet would also provide the greatest leverage to lash back and do enough harm to disarm their would be attackers. Out of nowhere, a shot rang out, and a third boy held the smoking revolver. "Killin' jest fills up the cemetery. No one learns not to kill by bein' killed 'cause he ain't here any more to learn. Let's give the old duffers a chance. Their bearing shows that they been where we are." From that point on the two seniors briefed them about what they had seen in Europe and Asia in the span of the two wars and the gangster years between them. They also bespoke the feelings of dread before battle and the despair when it was over to have killed a man over a clod of dirt or how kids were expected to lay down their lives for a fatherland or motherland without living to experience the nurturance offered by such bland statements as "Uncle Sam takes care of his own." The boys listened to what was said. They debated the issues, questioned the veracity and reality of what they had just heard. In the last analysis communication was generated where assumptions and errors in thought had prevailed in the dialogue. The rock and knife were freely given as mementos for the museum. They were also encouraged to work on their parents to request that the paddleboat and submarine visit their harbor.

The Clippingbirds also experienced some learning episodes on Mindanao, in the Philippine chain of islands. This island is known for its link to primeval times. The peculiar mix of war planes and people living like cavemen had generated oddities in thought that had combined these two anachronisms into the bizarre idea that men came to attack and tear apart the tribalism from the belly of a big bird that laid explosive eggs. Contact was to be avoided with these birdmen for they were evil spirits and were to be viewed as predators, harmful to the natural setting of the tribe.

The island was settled by four sampans in the year 1640. One of the ships did not want to settle in the area and moved on. They joined the crews of pirates in the Pacific plundering between the islands. They became the Dondara. The other two sampans settled on the island. One boatload found fertile areas, and some settled into an agrarian way of life. Others became fishermen. The other boatload did not like the plethora of rules that one community adopted as standards and went to the mountains to become hunters. Though in communities apart from one another, they each supplied foodstuffs and other goods to each other. They were also both plundered by the Dondara. This union of hunters, farmers and fishermen were known as the Drani. As the competition between farmers became too keen, some of them drifted off into making trinkets for trade with other islands and amongst themselves, as well as manufacturing weapons to defend themselves. Thus, had they existed for centuries. The invasion by the Japanese introduced modern warfare and weaponry to the island, and many weapons were stolen from them, including dynamite.

Donny, Becky, and their kids were part of a tow group to the Philippines and were enthralled with the independent living of the Drani. They and a couple of other tourists were attracted by the friendliness and were extended an invitation to live with them for a while by their chief, Tagura Brintas. The group of isolates accepted the invitation. One of the tour guides was a Dondara and told the pirates that these tourists had planned to live with the Drani. The greed manifested itself. The leader reasoned that the island could be raided, and the tourists could be held for ransom.

Donny and his family and the others made friends with the Drani. The children played together. The whole village pitched in to help build shelters for the newcomers, the former tourists took part in growing the food and tilling the fields, went out in the fishing boats, took part in the hunts, and helped clean the fish and game. Becky and the other women also took part in the cooking and washing clothes in the ocean. One day Donny noticed two large sampans pulling up to the harbor at the beach. He asked Tagura about them. Tagura explained about the Dondara and their periodic raids. He also informed him about them holding foreign prisoners for ransom. They also noticed that one was turning southward. Tagura explained that this ship was probably going south to steal the hunters' game and drive up to the beach and conquer the others.

Donny suggested a tribal meeting to develop a defense plan. The plan that was developed was a four pronged one: 1) That night barriers would be erected and weapons gathered. Practice sessions with these implements took place. The villagers would withdraw to the forest surrounding the village. Women and children would fight from the trees dropping dynamite, rocks, coconuts on the assailants. While the pirates struggled with the barriers part of the village men would attack and drive them to the woods, where they would face the rest, armed with spears, burning rags and dynamite. 2) Becky, one tourist, and Tagura would go south to warn the mountaineers of the pending attack and set up an ambush of the sailors going through the mountains. 3) Donny and three other men would go south and capture the sampan, abandoned by the pirates ,who went into the mountains. 4) Donny and one other man would bring up the stolen sampan and fill the hold of its lifeboat(s) with dynamite, steer it toward the remaining sampan, and blow it up while the sailors were engaged on land.

With the coming of dawn, the pirates left their ship and brought 2 cannons with them, which they set up on the beach. They fired one and were surprised that there was no response. As a precaution, they decided to approach the village from the perimeters at either end. They found a herd of elephants and lions (attracted to the meat laid down on the ground). After this were pits that had fires started in them. Behind this were sticks of dynamite, bound together waiting for the plunger connected to them to be pushed (which it was). This was followed by men rushing out of nowhere flinging spears and flaming spears at them. They ran for the woods where they were greeted by the same thing from behind trees, from which rocks, coconuts, sticks of lit dynamite, and insect nests were thrown on them. Those that survived surrendered. In the mountains, the sailors entered a cave that they thought would be a shortcut to the mountain village. Instead, they found an army armed the same way the village up north waiting behind the rocks and on the ledges above them and around them. They surrendered without a shot being fired. The land war was over.

Donny and his three companions in arms found a skeleton crew left on the sampan. Most of them were sleeping and killed with a slash to the throat. The guards on duty were attacked from behind and thrown overboard. Donny collected his share of the dynamite and tied all the sticks together. He sent two men back in the proa. When he and his partner got to the other boat, they lowered the lifeboat of dynamite and aimed it at the other sampan, then blew it out of the water. On the way home, the prisoners were put on an island far away from Mindanao and left to fend for themselves.

The night of celebration was to be the last night the Clippingbirds spent with their new friends. They sang and danced with them, drank their homemade brew, exchanged gifts, and accepted the gift of the sampan that was left; it was put in the museum. Bobby and Becky said they'd return and would bring the museum boats with them.

Dominic, Penny, and Chris got along famously, but Dominic was plagued by nightmares. He never had to fight in a foreign war, but what he had to deal with in the turf fights with Spanish people and with Blacks proved every bit as harrisome as Iwo Jima and Guadalcanal. He endured nightmares at night. They were sometimes low moans, sometimes shouting out of fear or anger, sometimes confined to gnashing of teeth, sometimes they were breaking out in sweats. When Penny asked him about it, he couldn't remember anything. Together they went to a hypnotist. Then she heard the whole thing.

Dominic was born in Sicily and lived in the same village as the local Don. His surname was Umbriano, closely related to the word for drunk. His father was indeed an alcoholic. He could not hold down a job and would frequently blame his hard lot in life on his wife and son. His blame took the form of beatings to both of them. Dominic was only six when he found a heavy lead pipe and hid it at home. Despite his drinking, Pieto (the father) was a favorite of the Don because he was a loyal soldier and would do whatever assignment came his way, be it to kill, rob, beat, kidnap, or maim. On the day Dominic brought home the pipe, Pieto had had a tough assignment from his Don. The Don, who was married, had gotten one of the village doxies pregnant and wanted the pregnancy terminated, which she refused to do. The soldier had to locate an abortionist and go with him to the lady's house and administer the abortion with or without her consent. The struggle was violent and ended with her attempting to stab Pieto. Reflexively he shot her to death before she got to him. He had to have a drink after that and came home drunk. His anger at himself was at its peak, and he needed a scapegoat. His wife came to the door to greet him, hoping to find him in a good mood. Instead, he knocked her to the floor, pounced on her, and hit her face until blood came gushing through her mouth. Dominic heard the sounds of teeth and bones being broken. He got his pipe and hit his father until he bled from his eyes. Staggering to avoid the blows of the pipe, he fell down the hallway stairs and broke his neck.

Now the Don was looking for the boy. Before he ran for his life, he made sure his mother was taken care of. She lived, and they decided to leave the country and move in with her sister in Brooklyn. On the way to the dock in Palermo, one of the Don's lieutenants recognized mother and child; he phoned the Don who instructed him to follow and eliminate them before they reached New York. They were both aware of him and what his task was. She approached the soldier to let her son live and had to agree to meet him in one of the lifeboats every night for a sexual encounter to extract this promise from him.

One night Dominic's mother woke him up in trying to keep her rendezvous, and he followed her. He kept his distance and didn't see too much, but he recognized his Mother's cries of pain and heard the lieutenant's derisive laughter. He saw him light a cigar and put it out on her arm. He heard her scream again. He knew his mother and why she would endure such abuse. He decided to act. During the day he followed the lieutenant and observed him getting tipsy at the bar. He stopped at the ship's rail to catch a breath of air. Dominic pushed him over the rail into the sea below. He hollered for help and that he couldn't swim. He was rescued and was suspicious of Dominic after that. One night before his mother could get up for their meeting, Dominic went to the lifeboat with a can of gasoline he had stolen from the ship's fuel stores, tripped him so that he fell into the boat, poured the gasoline on him, and lit a match. He stuck one of the soldier's cigarettes into his victim's mouth and lit this also. His mother never found out what happened to the man. He had been a stowaway and was not listed as a passenger.

After landing in New York and finding his aunt in Brooklyn, Dominic got a real exposure to street life. The schools were houses of violence; stealing was a way of life. Different nationalities, races, and brotherhoods teemed the neighborhoods. Gang wars decided what turf belonged to whom. Belonging to a gang was a sign of protection and honor. This honor, as well as trust was earned by showing loyalty, no matter what was asked. In fact, this gang loyalty replaced family loyalty because the family was old timers, who only knew the ways of the old country. Gangs who tried to take the turf of the gang in that neighborhood suffered violent acts; killing was not out of the question. Gangism and gang terror spread to other cities and other states. The senseless beating and maiming of old people or weak kids, forced sex with females, and people that innocently found their ways to the neighborhood or other gangs that came there got to Dominic. He believed that America was supposed to be free. People were supposed to go wherever they wanted, as long as they did not harm anyone and minded their own business.

The crowning shame came when he was given the assignment to eliminate a Black male youth and a Puerto Rican girl, who were interfering with the neighborhood drug trade by trying to buy reefer from one of their own dope boys and take it back to their neighborhoods.

They were held prisoner in an empty warehouse. At midnight Dominic was to take them out and shoot them, then dump the bodies in the river outside of the Massachusetts state line. He went to the warehouse early and slugged the guard over them with a pipe he found in the trash. He then cut them loose and told them to get out of there.

After they left, he slugged himself in the head with the pipe. The escape was suspiciously regarded, but no one could prove anything. After the prisoners escaped from Andorra, he had to break with the mob, and they were after him. However, Scherlien intervened on his behalf, and he was not bothered. Others, with higher ambitions, had longer memories; they were plotting to eliminate both Scherlien and Dominic.

Chapter 3

The result was that a meeting was called in a suburb of Boston. The chief of the faction that wanted a change was consiglieri for the family. He called the meeting without letting Scherlien or Dominic know about it. An informer who wanted to retire from the mob told her about it, and a deal was made with the federal government and Craine, along with Scherlien and Dominic. The two mobsters were granted immunity from prosecution for telling the FBI about the meeting and put on 10 years probation which was served by working for the museums as a community service. Many gangsters that were wanted for a long time were apprehended, and the pair was instrumental in providing information that carried long prison sentences due to the information that was given. They also were given new names and new locations in which to live.

Scherlien and Bobby and Penny and Dominic had a double wedding. The mob looked at this as an opportunity to wipe out both of the traitors, and several of them showed up at the wedding. One of them took a shot at Dominic and hit him in the chest. He was still standing and looked down and saw the bullet in his tie clasp. The thug took aim again then dropped with blood spurting from his neck. Mictal was standing holding a smoking gun with a silencer attached. Penny ran up to him and hugged him, saying, "You saved my man's life. I want you to be Godfather to our baby, and I'm naming her/him after you." She then kissed his cheek and went back to her husband, and smilingly whispered, "You rascal, I'm pregnant." He smiled back and said, "That's what you get for flaunting yourself at me." She said, "Wait till later."

Ms. Pitressin and her Principal husband were there. She snubbed Chris because of his illegitimacy; Donny saw this and walked over to them with anger in his eyes. "Hello, you're looking prosperous. That might not be the case if you don't acknowledge your grandson and provide for him. Ms. Pitressin visually shook and turned red. Then she turned to her daughter and grandson, as well as Dominic. The principal held out his hand for a handshake, and Donny looked at it as if it were a piece of fecal matter and gave him a Bronx cheer.

A piece of teamwork was set up that brought the FBI more captives. Scherlien called in to let the government know that thugs had shown up at her wedding, and she told them where to wait to round them up. Craine went to get his plane. The seating was now outside, to prepare for the departures of the new couples. Arrangements were made to seat all the gangsters together, so that Craine would know where to strafe. When the flowers and garters were thrown, they were caught by two mobsters. Maybe they enjoyed the bliss of matrimony in jail. The bullets directed the gangsters to a woods nearby, where they walked into the arms of the FBI.

Chapter 4

Rodin was startled as he walked through the door to his house. His wife came storming down the stairs waving a newspaper at him. In fact, she almost put his eye out. He heard her yell something like ricking or rigging. He saw a picture from the past, and his jaw almost dropped off as he recognized the face of so long ago when he and a German man were looking at Liana's legs as she danced. He had coaxed him out of the Parisienne bar into an alley with German drinking songs and stuck a knife in his throat. His name was Baron Richtling, and his family was a powerful, wealthy family from Prussia. He had served with Rommel in Africa and was wounded badly in the leg and had to leave the service. His family had made money during the war in a mattress factory. They did not know what had happened to him until his skeleton was found in a field next to a decaying building that used to be a bar. A family ring on what was left of his finger identified him. They were launching an investigation to find out what the circumstances of his death were. Rodin and Liana had a long talk. They hired a dual team of lawyers. They were Bobby and Bruno Havelich.

The first part of the defense was to investigate defects of character in the baron, himself. While investigating his tour in Africa, Bobby happened upon some information that linked Richtling to a woman from a Berber tribe. Apparently she had died in childbirth in a Tunisian village in 1942. Bobby found in his information search that this was at about the time that Rommel was in the area and at a time when Jews, that were to later to become Sephardic Jews in Israel, still lived in Africa to avoid the European pogroms. The mother of such a Jewish girl was captured and interned at Bergen Belsen. She escaped to Andorra and smuggled herself to Nigeria on a Spanish freighter and spent the rest of the war in Lagos, where she now resided. In the late part of 1941, a drunken German officer with a bad leg came to their village and raped a young lady, who was among some Jewish prisoners about to be sent to concentration camps. When Bobby visited in her in Lagos, with the newspaper article and picture, she identified the man in the picture as the rapist and gave him a written, notarized statement that she would testify to the fact in a hearing if one was held.

The second part of gathering the evidence also proved to be one of digging up nasty, discrediting truths proved to involve ugly facts about the plaintiff. The family had made a fortune by taking over the mattress factory of a Jewish family that had been deported to a concentration camp at Treblinka. They had gotten news of this ahead of time and bribed an official to let them leave the country in a ship headed to Ceylon (now Sri Lanka). They took their ownership papers with them because they knew their God could not allow such an unholy movement as Nazi-ism to survive. From Ceylon, they took another ship to Israel, which they believed would be their homeland someday. The family now lived near the Wailing Wall. Bobby now interviewed remnants of this family and had pictures of the ownership papers, accompanied by a notarized statement that the company was not sold to the Richtlings or any one else. One more tidbit of information would be gathered and verified by the defense group.

The Richtling family had made no secret about their loyalty to Hitler, but some of their contracts were not public knowledge. Bruno brought his expertise in these matters, and he went further than his knowledge to secure damning facts and evidence. The name of the Berber girl, who had died in childbirth, was secured via hospital records, and that her mother was at Bergen Belsen was verified by records obtained from Elie Wiesenthal, the Israeli investigator. He was also retained to verify contracts between the Richtlings and Treblinka, Bergen Belsen, Majdanek, and several others for shipment of mattress materials to the family in return for a cut rate on mattresses that the family shipped back. Sworn statements were obtained that mattress materials consisted of ground up body parts and body hair from deceased prisoners. Small portions of the stuffing were stolen by prisoners and sent to Mr. Wiesman after the war. The hair and other stuffing were sent to labs for analysis and tested positive for residue from the gas used in the showers for extermination purposes.

All this data was compiled and put in a safe in the lawyers' office, and also given to the La Monde family to be used at a later date if needed. Raoul, seeking revenge communicated with the Richtlings, and via the family attorney, a meeting was arranged. The family was charging Rodin with murder and Liana with complicity. In light of the information presented to the family, the investigation was dropped with a signed statement that it would not be brought up again by the family.

Bringing up this episode from the past began to play on Rodin's mind, and he began to ruminate about other behaviors being reawakened. He began to experience repetition of these thoughts at bedtime and did not share them with Liana because he did not want to worry her. He began to talk about them in his sleep and to agonize about some of their past behaviors. There was a groaning quality about some of his utterings. When he would still not be drawn into discussing his feelings, Liana began to push him to go and see their son Randal, to see if anything was physically wrong. He made an appointment reluctantly.

He opened up just as reluctantly to his son. Randal had detected an abnormality in his heartbeat and insisted on x-rays. He did explain that by keeping awake, his father was making his heart work harder, and that it was beating faster. He prescribed some sleeping medication. In two days, the x-rays came and showed an occluded ventricular vein and a defective ventricular valve. Randal visited them that night and discussed diet, a regimen of activity and activity limits, and a prescription for nitroglycerin, plus regular visits. He told his father in no uncertain terms: "You're my father, and I'd like you around a while. I'll try a week to get that vein to open, and the same week to get the valve to heal, then it's the surgeon's knife or your ass by my hand. Got it?" Rodin agreed, but he grumbled because he knew it limited sex. Liana smacked his shoulder.

Rodin came, at last, to realize that the hatred to which his family had clung was pointless. He was at a bus station and saw a French couple in the midst of a heated argument over whether or not Quebec should secede from Canada and join itself to France, the real forefathers of Democracy, not like the phony Brits that preached their doctrines of equality and had practiced sheer racism in India. The man added that the so-called egalitarian French spoke a good game and practiced despotism, as well as racism, in Vietnam. They got so agitated that they stopped talking to each other. Their scurrilous voices stopped, and the rapid, loud, French nasal sounds stopped with them.

Suddenly a disheveled man with a bloody face and blood on his shirt came up to the couple and began pleading with them to give him bus fare to Quebec City because he had just been robbed by a gang and had no way to get back there. They told him to go to the police and shook their heads that a fellow Quebecker had to resort to begging to get sufficient funds and began their argument in French again. At that point, Rodin introduced himself to the man. He called his wife at home and said he was bringing someone he met home to dinner because he had something to discuss with her, related to him.

During the ride to his house, Rodin found out the man's name was Rousseau L'Otteur. He was born in Chicago and left home for Quebec when he was 18 because he wanted to avoid the draft during the Vietnam War. He was also of French descent and sick of people making fun of his name. He claimed to be from the Ottawa tribe and had lost an ancestor in the French and Indian War, who had gone deaf and was shooting his own men. Rodin asked what the name of this ancestor was, and Russ (as he called himself) said it had to do with an otter. Rodin asked if it could not be Lonely Otter. The reply was that it may have been. Rodin quickly told Russ his family history and that his interchange with the French couple had awakened an interest in going back where the whole thing started and building a family tree. In fact, he had gotten the idea of discussing the trip with his wife and could use their taking him home as an excuse for going back there. Now they could build the tree together.

Liana was enthusiastic about the idea, and they started their trip that weekend. Rousseau stayed at their home and left with them. Russ had some peculiarities to which they had to adjust. For instance, he could not pass a drawer without opening it and emptying it of contents useful to him. On his first night, he ransacked Liana's jewelry drawer and took a pearl necklace.

They started out driving from Pittsburgh across Pennsylvania to New York State. They stopped at Albany and got separate rooms. Liana turned to her husband with a newly awakened desire. She could not lie still under him. Afterwards he asked her what had so moved her, and she said that she had been waiting ever since their first night for him to dispel his hatred of France, and now he was returning to its source. He kissed her gently and said, "I was beginning to be eaten up by hatred. Now I want to forget it. We have a beautiful son and soon will have beautiful grandchildren. How can a hate filled creature help little ones find their ways in the world?" She kissed him again. They went to Russ' room to invite him go have dinner with them. They ordered venison steaks with a pasta side dish and home grown tomatoes. They had ordered a couple bottles of wine with lemon meringue pie for dessert. Russ and Rodin were so excited about starting the family tree that they immediately went to the nearest library after dinner and began the process of research. They discovered that after Lonely Otter had left the French army in his disgrace, he no longer saw himself as worthy of his Odawa tribe and went to the west to live alone on a mountain for the rest of his days. He wandered further and further South and crossed the border into Mexico where he sat dejected and exhausted, waiting for the Spaniards to kill him.

Instead a pretty, pert dancer approached him and tugged at him until he joined in her dancing around the room, displaying her body as she moved. She saw the pain in his eyes and stroked his cheek as she moved close to him. They could not communicate a word, but she saw that this was a man who suffered the heartache of the damned. She took him to her bed and loved him passionately until she saw the hurt look soften. Then she let him sleep and slept herself. She knew he was a good man and that she would join him no matter where he went. She went with him to their mountain and built a house with their own hands. She bore him three sons and a daughter that figured into the history of the Midwest. They were: Red Otter, Otter Hide, Leaping Otter, and Dancing with Otter. He stayed by himself and joined no tribe. When his sons and daughter were old enough, he took them to meet Tecumseh.

This installment started the family history. Further installments were added at other stops, but the major impetus came in Quebec. Russ felt a pang of guilt and put the necklace in the glove compartment of the car. He forgot his habit, and nothing was ever stolen from the La Mondes by him again.

Tecumseh did not trust either the British or the Americans. During the Revolutionary War a tribe that wanted to get along with the white man had converted to Christianity. They were the Delawares in southeastern Ohio. Both sides were so engrossed in their war that they wiped out this tribe. Though he knew that both of these white warriors were imperialistic, Britain was not pushing the Native Americans to the periphery of settlement, where the game was scarce and the soil was poor. Therefore, he decided to support England, who was trying to contain Napoleon Bonaparte by sea. The Americans attempted to trade with their old ally, and Britain attempted to suppress this move by boarding American ships and drafting the American sailors as British subjects, as if there had been no revolution.

Lonely Otter's progeny followed suit with Tecumseh's preference without realizing that the whole purpose was to give the Pan Indian a chance to develop so that the Indians would become culturally unified and stand before the white man as a force to be reckoned and bargained with. Thus, they put their whole effort towards aiding a British victory. The men directed their efforts towards supplying manpower, munitions, and weapons to the English, while their sister pursued a more logistic plan. She attempted to negotiate with Jean La Fitte and the Cajuns to support the British and the Seminoles to form an army to march northwest and engage the Americans at New Orleans. However, she did not take into account the slyness and military awareness of Andy Jackson or the drive of a young midshipman, named David Farragut. The Americans won the War of 1812. La Mondes fought on both sides in this war.

Likewise, they fought in the expansionist wars involving Texas and Mexico and reflected the sectionalism of the regions in which they lived. This sectionalism was also expressed in the American Civil War, as La Mondes spilled their blood at Bull's Run, Antietam, Shiloh, Chickamauga, and Gettysburg. La Mondes also froze with Napoleon

Bonaparte in Russia and joined Frenchmen crying for a republic. Previous to this, they led the wealthy to the guillotine and clamored later for removal of Napoleon II after he was soundly defeated by Bismarck, whom he had let goad him into a losing war. This led to the family's handling the defaming of the French empire, so expertly managed by Rodin and, later Rodin and Liana, in the two world wars and in Africa and Asia after these debacles.

Rodin was beginning to feel a sense of contentment and fulfillment that he was beginning to see that the hatred which had engulfed him had led to more destruction. He could feel the hate ebbing out of him. He went to his home and, after opening the door, he saw his wife bent over picking up the pieces of a broken glass. He sneaked up behind her and reached inside her skirt and began to caress her thighs. She stood up with a startled squeak and laughed. He picked her up and carried her upstairs, where they undressed each other and made passionate love until they fell asleep in each others' arms.

In the morning, Liana woke up with a smile and nudged her husband to get the smile off of his face. It would not budge. She felt his pulse and found none. He had died in his sleep. Liana wept and called Randal. He pronounced him dead.

The next day the funeral was held, and Liana cried uncontrollably. She went to live with her son and wife and grandchildren. Russ consoled her as a friend and began an endless flirtation with her that was both flattering and annoying. However, she kept on with the family tree, and carried the work on with the museum with the assistance of Patrick and Craine, who spoke about his efforts in both wars as heroic. They also agitated the French government to recognize his heroism, despite his negative efforts toward their imperialism.

Chapter 5

The brunt of waging the peace fell to Donny, Craine, and Patrick, Donny was not warlike in the sense of not having participated in the world wars, Korea, or Vietnam, but his relentless energy had gone to find a weakness in the white man, as the Caucasian found in the Red man and exploit it, as the white man had done. Craine had experienced violence almost from the start when he had to attack another family to defend his own. This was complicated by World War I participation and his postwar associations with gangsters. These connections colored his behaviors so that he achieved positive results by using gangland techniques, which added a dimension of horror to what he achieved. Pat, on the other hand, was born in the wake of violence and tried to establish a peaceful format to enter the art of problem solving. However, the violence of his forebearer and the contempt his contemporary held for white hypocrisy often made peaceful solutions difficult to achieve.

Scherlien and Bobby did not want any notoriety, obviously because of the role their infamy played in their previous relationships. They lived in Roanna, Nevada, a small suburb outside of Las Vegas under the name of Mr. and Mrs. Louis Barringer. He specialized in publishing law and was earning a good living. As a side business, they bought a storefront and went into the business of changing foreign monies into American money. A Bulgarian gentleman moved a few doors from them and was very interested in opening up a laundry next to their store. He gave his name as Anatolo Boganti. The Clippingbirds noticed that a lot of men would come to his house in the wee hours of the morning, and that he would have a lot of Bulgarian money to exchange for dollars the next day.

They did not want any involvement with the federal government and asked Craine to find out what he could about the man. It turned out that Anatolo was really Bulgarian, but he was a member of the Russian Mafia. He was part of a gang that received jewels and artwork that were stolen from fences in different European nations and paid for in Bulgarian coin, which was converted to American money. The American currency was then counterfeited and used to pay losses at one particular casino, a casino that Mr. Boganti wanted to go broke so that it could be bought by the Russian Mafia at a cheap price because the Bulgarian would report the counterfeiting to the treasury department.

Craine had conferred with Donny, and they had devised a dual scheme. Donny would send in a shill dealer to change the losses to wins and pay them off with the counterfeit money, then report the winner as giving them counterfeit money when they had lost. This was not good enough for Craine, who wanted the lesson to be permanent. He found out the room numbers of the Mafioskis and sent his own mobsters there to rough up the Bulgars, or whatever nations they represented. One room had three armed men in it. Since gunsels know only one way to prevent getting roughed up, a shootout took place, and two men were killed. The other got away. In order to not get hunted down, he put himself under federal protection in a penitentiary.

A member of the Winters gang was incarcerated there. Consequently, Craine went there to visit him. He had a lot of pull in the prison and called a meeting of the Irish prisoners. One was friendly with the Mafioso group, who were backing one of their younger members to get a position in the honor camp, so he could go into the community and learn a trade. The Bulgar made friends easily, and he was also young in years. His friends kept pushing him to vie for the position. The Irishers paid off the guards that were in charge of selection for the honor camp, and the Mafioski got the position. The Italians were angered and set up an accident in the auto body shop, in which a car fell off of the lift while the Bulgar was working on it. He was killed instantly.

The FBI was suspicious of the circumstances of the death and began investigating. They met with both the Italian and Irish nationality groups and used sentence reduction or complete freedom as bribes to snitch. They looked at the relationships among the residents and sources of cooperation and rivalry and divisiveness between the two groups. They could trace the sources to those that associated with the Bulgar, but they came to a stumbling block and couldn't find anyone outside the prison associated with the crime.

The Irishers and Italians became silent because they knew what fate would await them if they cooperated with the authorities. In fact, the Irishman and the Italian who had communicated with each other were mysteriously killed. But active participants are not the only sources of information in a prison: Isaac Delfino was in the Italian clique. He was never fully accepted because he was Jewish. His mother died in childbirth, and his father was embittered by this. Since he was the child whose birth caused his mother's death, he was hated by his father. The father would find excuses to beat him and belittle his achievements, to make fun of his ways of talking and walking, as well as his mannerisms in front of his brothers and sister. Isaac took this for years. At the age of twenty, his father was kicking him at a time when he had just finished his work shift in a factory and was bone tired. Isaac picked up a hot iron from the ironing board and slammed his father in the face with it.

He was sentenced to twenty years for manslaughter. However, he hated authority to such an extent that he kept getting years added to his sentence for assaulting and seriously injuring guards that made fun of his heritage or for anything. that irritated him. He also learned that he could control the inmates by observing their activities and keeping records of them, which he kept hidden. This included not only inmates but also staff, including the warden. He had noticed that since the time of Craine's visit to the Winters gang member, more huddled meetings took place on both the Italian and Irish groups, and the violence had begun.

He was getting tired of prison life and was plotting to see if the state would knock time off of his sentence in return for a little exchange of information. He brought together toughs from both sections to question the incarcerated gang member. From what Isaac was able to deduce, Craine somehow had maneuvered to have the Mafioski killed.

Isaac had enough protection so that he could openly ask about the gang connections, and he also had arranged the transfer of all information to the authorities if anything would happen to him. He also had a documentary of Craine's activities during prohibition and his role in rescuing the prisoners from Andorra. He even had a photograph of the plane that Craine had used to strafe the Mafiosos and had signed testimony from Tandry that this was the same plane that had strafed the Ornams, wiping them out. In fact he had pulled all his information together and set a meeting up with the FBI.

Copies were sent to Mictal's relatives, who were a Senator and Congressman. They also began to contact Isaac to get what information they could. They once again began to pester Mictal, who went straight to Donny with the data. Donny engaged Bruno and his brother to receive the data and to create a defense case out of it.

Scherlien and Penny had a good rapport with young people, and Bobby and Dominic had a lot of information under their belt about flaws in the legal system that young people were hungering to correct and to present to their classes. Law students were notorious for looking for this information to present for brownie points to their professors. Between the four of them, they organized a group of students to correspond with prisoners, then start visiting them and picking up bits of information that could be used. For example, they found out that one could get into the ventilating system through the fan system on the roof at the prison by stopping the fan temporarily, and that there were no guards at that spot between 1:00-3:00 A.M. During these hours Isaac would go to a room connected to the ventilating system, pry loose a board in the wall, and take and study his papers that bore blackmail available literature that put him in control of others. The law students had been landing on the roof via a helicopter and observed this process the week before Isaac was to meet with the FBI. They got the information to Bobby, who came with them with a flashlight and camera. He lowered himself into the room, took whatever pictures he needed, made changes that would ruin Isaac's credibility, and left with the rest of the crew into the waiting helicopter. The case to have the sentence reduced was blown wide open. Isaac was furious and vowed revenge.

He knew that Craine was involved, and the only ways he could get even would be to strike at him through his health, age, and anxiety for his family's welfare. He had henchmen in the community through the Mob that tampered with his, his wife's, and his son's cars, damaged garage doors so that they would fall on someone, installed electrical appliances so that they would blow up and start fires, had delivered food items poisoned or injected with salmonella and other bacteria. The toll was beginning to be paid with Craine's sleeplessness and worry causing him to have an increased heart rate and blood pressure.

Pat took him to the doctor, and medication was prescribed. Molly saw that he stuck to his diet, took him on walks, saw to it he took his medication, and fussed over him the way a wife fusses over her husband, who is old and having health problems. Some of the anxiety provoking problems were traced to the mob and back to Isaac. He was no spring chicken, and Craine had his own contacts both in and outside of the prison. Thus began a war of nerves. It appeared that Isaac won this war. Fearing a lawsuit, the parole board released Isaac to parole to Jamaica. He died by choking while eating a taco that had a button in it. The waiter was one of the luggage loaders in Craine's and Pat's airline, who had been unionized by the strike Craine and Bugsy Moran had "supervised" in the twenties.

Craine and Molly had gone to a movie about an Irish immigrant that became a fighter in barehanded pick up fights to earn money and got into union brawls then into gang activity. When they left the theater, a boy drew a knife and held it to his throat, demanding money. Molly was petrified and told him to give it to him. He reached into his back pocket, but noticed the young man had a tremor in his eye. He said to the youth: "I grew up doing what you're trying, and it led me to some sorry days; how'd you like to be my gardener instead." The youth was touched, but could not separate himself from his macho ego. "Don't try to talk your way out of this with slick talk. I'm not afraid to cut your gizzard out. My family needs pampers and food." Seeing an opening, Craine tripped him and quickly grabbed the knife. "Asshole, I'm trying to give you a chance to pay your way without a jail sentence. For the last time, take it or leave it. Now I've got the knife." The young man looked like he had the fight knocked out of him. Craine helped him up, and he hit Craine in the head with a rock and ran. Molly got his cell phone out of his pocket and called 911. The paramedics stopped the bleeding, but the flurried motion had started chest pains, and her husband had to be rushed to Intensive Care. She and Pat and Randi spent an anxious night in the hospital.

The boy was caught and was now asking Craine for a job. In anger, Pat told him his job was to straighten out while he was locked up. Through Craine he got a job in the institution, and his wages were sent to his girlfriend and baby. The robbery knife was sent to the museum.

The boy's father came to visit Craine on behalf of his son. He wanted Craine to drop the charges. Craine tried to explain that he did not file the charges. The youth was apprehended with a knife in his hand and the robbery attempt was obvious by the condition in which he had left the couple. He did offer to renew the job offer after the sentencing was done and offered to help the youngster get competent legal representation.

The man had neglected his son and was feeling guilty about it. He had left his wife when the boy was small, due to finding her impossible to get along with. The boy missed his father and bullied his mother as a consequence. He was a frequent visitor to court, due to his unmanageability. On top of that, he had gotten a girl pregnant just to prove to himself that he had a functional penis, which may have established a connection with his cerebrum, if there was one. The robbery attempt put the clincher on what his plans would be for the next two years, at least.

In a flurry of rage, the father tore loose the IV providing Craine with nourishment and medication. The man ran out of the room right into the arms of the police. Before he fell into unconsciousness, Craine screamed out, and Molly and Pat came running. Molly ran for the nurse, while Pat tried to administer CPR, then get his father on the bed once breathing had started. The IV was hooked up again, but Craine remained in a coma. Pat and his mother watched him round the clock. After three days, Craine died in his sleep.

The Mikawber clan had diminished considerably, but they and Malkia's family were there to send off Craine to his reward. Pat spoke about how his father had righted the wrongs to his family and his close friends and then helped others to find the right paths or to protect them so that they could. He had deliberately sought out those that been dealt cruel blows by life and tried to push them into a healthy re-start. Randal La Monde, Scherlien, Penny Pitressin, Bobby Clippingbird, Dominic Umbriano all testified how Craine, who did not bargain with the forces of evil, had saved their lives. He was compared to a latter day Robin Hood. The union worker that worked as a trucker and later at the airport loader testified that Craine had saved him and his family from starvation.

Section VI

Donny's Trial

Chapter 1

Donny realized that he was the only one of the three men that had let anger turn to hatred that was left. He knew that his wife had been wanting him to put this behind him for her and the children's sakes for years. One theme had pervaded his thinking for years: the white man had discovered that the Red man had a weakness for alcohol that was used to render him powerless in the endless battle for the greed for his land. To establish that the Indian Culture was one to be reckoned with, as the plan formulated by Tecumseh stated, Donny decided to find the white man's weakness, his greed for money. With this in view, Donny became a mogul in the gambling industry and controlled who won or lost, dependent upon whether or not he decided they were his enemies.

Together with his wife's pushing, Donny had the teachings of two forbearers to guide him, and they did when he had twinges of conscience.

He remembered his father's telling him about the Battle of Remagen when his battalion had to fight kids to get from France into Germany. He had to program himself to see them as the enemy so that he could fight to kill. For a while he had a hard time viewing them as kids again after the war, but he had to reconstruct his psyche so that he could relate to marry and have a family. The second part of the twinge was his father's chauffeur, Ki. He had encountered difficulty in the war with his Japanese origin keeping him from being accepted as an American soldier until he had gotten support from Ira Hayes and Guy Gabaldon to remind the GI's what their ideals for the war were. He also thought about his family adventure in Mindanao, in which he and his family had helped a tribe from being controlled by another tribe and some pirates. He had thoughts about returning there and helping the two tribes and pirates put their differences behind them and work for the common good. This went beyond the Pan Indian Movement and was meant to develop a format for all three factions to establish an orderly relationship.

Becky pointed out that before they could do this, they would have to enhance communication skills with each other then work on how to get the three factions to communicate beyond their greed, feelings of insecurity, and mistrusts.

The project began with a twofold plan: Donny and Becky started taking communication classes at the university and took roles together in a local acting group, in which they would have to develop skills in how to talk and not talk successively. The other dimension of the plan was to communicate to Tagura, of the Drani, that they wanted to return and what they had in mind. This was done via the system of tourists and the guide system that was previously established. A second part of the plan was to inform Bobby and Bruno of what was occurring and to arrange for the sending of follow-up reports to them.

To give life to their learning, they enrolled in communication classes and took interacting roles in a local acting group. They took the classes as a family and got the kids roles in a kids' drama. They did this for six months and felt they were ready for their journey. They had contacted the American Embassy to arrange placement in Manila with a family so that the children could attend school during the week and be with them on Mindanao on the weekends. They also contacted Tagura through the guide system to let him know when they would arrive. The Dondara also were informed unintentionally by this guide system, as were the pirates. Donny and family took a plane to Manila, where they met Tagura and an enclave of guards. The couple bought a boat armed with a cannon and a harpoon gun at either end for any troublemakers to see. From there they sailed to Mindanao. The boat was docked and hidden in a place that was not obvious, but was easily moved in case of having to pursue anyone.

Tagura and Donny and Becky met to develop a strategy for bringing all three groups together. The first step was to list those that were pro union and those were anti- and to find steps to approach the pros-. Then they had to find issues behind which they would unite, as well as issues that would divide them.

Brontos Segovia served as a liaison to the Guide Committee. He was also a Dondara and did not like being spied upon by the pirates and always having his information questioned. Likewise, Captain Adalos did not like having to pay ships that did not go on raids a portion of his take to ensure that idle ships could purchase enough weapons to protect themselves. These two were brought before the meeting with Tagura by stealing the vessel out of the harbor after staging a phony meeting with the crew and the captain and getting them drunk and back aboard.

Tagura started out by telling both of the dissidents that they could eliminate their problems with the law and with people they preyed upon by fighting back if they became part of a legal framework, i.e. operating under the auspices of the Philippine Nation. He pointed out that by pooling their efforts the Dondara and the pirates could help provide historical realities to tourists via staging re-enactments, holding classes about real events, or asking actual participants in historical or present events to give talks. By so doing they could develop incomes for contributing, instead of having to create a network of defense for breaking laws that would only end in defeat of the perpetrators. There would be no need for spying if they all did essential work for the building of the country's economy. The jobs would be steady, and the need for backbiting spying would disappear.

Becky addressed the group by stating that every nation knows the bitterness of war. That Mindanao stood out as a monument for preserving the beauty that Man lived before knowing about bombs, guns, and terror to control populations was evident because people flocked to come to see it. That this persevered was evident by the way people came to see Williamsburg, Virginia which demonstrated how a colony at peace with itself was able to function. The monuments at Gettysburg and Antietam stressed the horror of war by stating the numbers killed. She openly asked why should this senselessness continue by factions fighting amongst themselves when the purpose of the war was to stop this?

Donny got on his feet with a shame faced grin on his face. He brought back the rage his youth threw in his face for the corruption, racism, public indifference, and downright shame of living on a reservation. He spoke of his resolve to demonstrate the Pan Indian Movement by introducing the white man's weakness of greed and controlling him with it, the way he had introduced the Red man's weakness, alcoholism to him and used it to control his advance. He further elaborated that the teachings of his wife, his father, and Ki helped him see that the cruelty of what he had endured left survivors that might not have been there to fight the way Martin Luther King Jr. and Ghandi had taught men to fight. Out and out war would have left a wake of destruction that may have paralleled Corregidor and Bataan, with no return of MacArthur. He added that being part of the Philippine Union was a way to create betterment for all without sacrificing some of that number. In the wake of this presentation, the two dissidents agreed to join forces with Tagura to present Mindanao as a piece of the Philippines that wanted to demonstrate to the world that we are all part of living together, and that this is combined with adding the knowledge we gain by our present endeavors and what we learned from ancestors about getting along with each other.

After it was over, Becky ran into his arms and held him to her. There were tears in her eyes. He smiled into her face and whispered into her ear, "If you want to cry now, wait till tonight." She laughed and hit him in the shoulder. But they had to close the windows that night.

In a strategic sense, Donny was laying groundwork for his own pending defense. However, he felt that he owed his compadres some defense for their actions, which were like the road to Hell, paved with good intentions. After all, they were all in the same ballgame.

He traced Craine's penchant for violence to the fact that he and his family were not allowed the basic human tenet of being different. Even the Church had to teach him a lesson for this sin, a lesson that did not frown on trying to slash an infant's and a woman's throat because his family persisted in worshipping God in their own way and without the restriction that they confine their love to their own religion, or the one dictated to them. Thus, the anger at criminality that was not held accountable created a person that fought back in kind. It took a good woman to wean him away from the eye for an eye mentation, but his way of getting things done came back to him when force was applied the same way, i.e. to shape him or mold him into someone else's way of thinking or acting. This information was given to Bruno and Bobby and confirmed by them by Pat and Molly.

In Rodin's case, the family history that had been created gave evidence that the La Mondes had basically fought for decency and justice both in America and Europe, but there was a jaundiced eye when it came to the French nation, that espoused giving birth to the concepts of liberty, brotherhood and equality, but practiced subjecting its colonials to the same demeaning, dehumanizing behavior that Nazis and Americans, as well, subjecting cultures they overran. The hypocrisy of this thinking began for the family with the deafening of Lonely Otter and persisted throughout the Vietnam War. Rodin was fighting for a family honor that had been submerged beneath the feet of a so-called progress that used another people, as if they were a thing.

Donny realized that cleaning up the actions of his predecessors in demanding revenge would add to his credibility in court. Hence, he made sure that the evidence he had gathered was sent to his lawyers with a way to substantiate any data that would be presented to the courtroom. Now he had to move on and build his own belief in his ability to change and to establish a means of making it believable to the culture wherein he resided and to the legal counterparts with which he was estimating he would have to deal.

Since we carry how we present ourselves where we live to where we go, Donny impressed upon his family that they had to protect Mindanao's image as a civilization from the past in how they related to their peers. Playing on computers, hanging around shopping malls, drag racing were all replaced by attending tribal hunts, swimming in rivers with members of the same sex with no clothing or swimming apparel. An added difficulty was that Ambler, Rambler, and Gambler were in the throes of late adolescence/young adulthood.

Ambler became enthralled by a young man that was a leader of the hunt. She watched him singlehandedly bag a boar after leading some compadres away from the main stream of the hunt, then preparing the carcass for slaughter and carting it back to their camp. His dark eyes and a shock of straight, jet black hair, agile movements, air of confidence, all began to attract her intensely. She started to follow him discreetly and learned where he went to wash clothing, bathe, and swim. She found out he was 19, as she was, and that his name was Bantu. She began to stray away from the protective, smothering watch of her two brothers and began to border on stalking behavior in her efforts to discover his comings and goings.

One day she discovered him washing an unusually large load of clothes by the river. She sat behind him on a flat rock and coughed to announce her presence. He whirled around to her, and his face flushed red with embarrassment at being seen at clothes washing. She laughed and touched his reddening visage. He explained that he was the sole support of his 6 younger brothers and sisters since his parents were kidnapped by the pirates and were being held for a ransom he was trying to earn. The recent kill of the boar had to be split between providing food and clothes for the family and going towards the payments sent to release his parents from the pirate stronghold.

Now when she looked into his eyes, she no longer saw the beauty of the agile hunter and boyish seducer of peers, but the pain of being forced to be a man when boyhood was supposed to be seeping its way out and manhood was supposed to be gradually moving in. She drew her face to his and kissed him lightly on the cheek. He hesitated shyly then drew her to him and kissed her fully on the lips. Together they finished washing the clothes and carried them to his dwelling, a cave between two copses of trees.

From then on they met at the riverbank. They held hands and talked about her plans, his plans, her brothers and his brothers and sisters, what their parents were like. The subject of the ransom was broached upon, and she suggested that her father might be able to help out via Brantos Segovia and Captain Adalos. She made a mental note to bring this issue up, but first, other issues had to be handled.

Ambler commented that the weather was warm and humid and, perhaps, Bantu would be more comfortable without his shirt; she began to pull It over his head. Their lips met, and he suggested that they move to more forested ground. He picked her up and carried her into a sheltered grove. She finished pulling his shirt off then began touching his skin on his chest and drew him to her. She slipped out of her shorts and thong then removed her halter. They ran to each other, completed the divestment of their remaining clothing, and began to touch and kiss all over. She thrust her breasts and lower lips to him and tugged and reached for his manhood. They touched and kissed each others nipples and mingled their tongues. She pulled him inside her, and they began to thrust together. The earth seemed to tremble and quake as they moved together, and in a crash and an almost volcanic roar, it quieted down. They breathlessly lay in each others arms. They went into the river, swam to each other, and washed the love from a few minutes before off of themselves. Love had begun.

Ambler told her father about the incident, and he responded with "Damn whites. They're eating everything that belongs to everyone else." He called a meeting between Tagura, Brantos, Captain Adalos, and the two young adults. Tagura began the meeting with a prayer that their old ways be safe in the forging ahead of the new nation. He also demonstrated that the teens of the community should take a stance on this issue. Both Adalos and Brantos agreed that the concordance should not be violated because too many would suffer from the sense of nationhood that would evolve in the wake of international understanding. With this statement an aura for noble purpose was started: Unite in brotherhood and build a nation of brothers. This meant that the brothers would have to protect and to police one another. Such a police action had to be done with such discretion, that the kidnappers would respect the others just because their rights would be in violation by the parties wronged.

With this said, the crew put their heads together and arrived at a plan they thought would be workable. Seventeen teenagers were to be trained in seamanship and steal three ships from the Pirates' Cove then hold the ships for ransom until the parents and other hostages were freed. Armed cannon were to be at the disposal of "the would be pirates," ready to fire from hidden points around the harbor.

They picked a night when all were celebrating in a night club and hadn't arrived back yet. When asked why the kids had to risk their lives, the first reason was that letting the adults do the reverse kidnapping would cause them to be watched more than if an outsider took the ships. A second reason was the concord would be a means of expansion without war and help to create a state, in which the population could assume a role in establishing a climate for growth.

Three men were assigned to bring her in. One man was in charge of the wheel, one had responsibility to man the guns. This meant cleaning, keeping stocked with ammo and supervising an order to fire. The other manned the sails and rudder. Their training was more basic than what they had expected. They were allowed enough time to get aboard, get the boats seaward, and get back to Mindanao.

Bantu did not like the idea. He felt that the relatives had to be responsible for bringing their families together again. His plan was to train all of the teens in seamanship and close quarters fighting for a period of six weeks then send them to the Pirates' Cove and capture more than half of the boats on a night when an excuse was given to call a meeting with the pirates and the guiding staff. The time he chose was Michaelmas Eve. Twelve out of nineteen ships were stolen. The following note was left at the pier where the ships were docked:

To those who Kidnap,
We need our relatives, as you need your ships. If all of the kidnapees are not returned to us in three days, we will return one destroyed ship a day until all twelve are destroyed or you decide to return them in good health. We will also make sure that the fact that you were brought to your knees by teenagers, not adults will be withheld from publication if you cooperate. We want the unification plan to help our nation prosper, but we are not a weak bunch of threatening kids. We mean business. If you cooperate with us no one need know that you were beaten by a bunch of kids.
Signed,
The Youth of Mindanao

Bantu's plan was unanimously approved, but Donny and the others were scared for these brave youth. Bantu's answer was that there came a time in the life of every youth when he/she had to grow up. Ambler's arm was linked to his, and her admiration and love showed in the glow of her face. The relatives were quickly returned. Pirates do not like to admit they are weak kneed. It makes their trade appear sissified.

Needless to say the plots to kidnap family members came to a sudden halt. Donny asked his wife to make sure that Ambler was well schooled in the arts of contraception. Becky assured him that this was done a long time ago.

Rambler and Gambler had free time on their hands since Ambler and Bantu had declared themselves. They began traveling around Mindanao and other islands, such as Luzon, Manila, and Zamboanga. On one occasion they separated, and this separation proved to be to their regret. Gambler was arguing with a peddler about the price of a necklace. Rambler looked up and saw a beautiful young lady making suggestive movements and moving closer to him. He moved toward her. Gambler looked up and saw him moving away. He stopped his haggling and went to Rambler. Because of the crowd, he got there too slowly. He connected with his brother in an alley. Both boys were surrounded by men wielding a short sword called kris. They were bound, gagged, and blindfolded. They were taken aboard a ship and docked at a port in southern Mindanao. They could feel themselves climbing toward mountainous country. They stopped before a cave and their blindfolds, but not their gags, were removed. A short man, whose physiognomy resembled the woman, stepped forward. She ran and hugged him and said, "Papa, I've brought you American guests."

"Hello, my name is Koutar, the sultan of the Mountain Moros. You are Americans, and your father is Donald Clippingbird; we hate Americans because their greed for land and money drove them here to steal our country. To do this they have allied themselves with the Christian Filipinos, who want to subjugate us by subjugating Allah. Your nation has caused us much mayhem and destruction. But we can also cause mayhem and destruction. Our Amoks and Juramentados are schooled to be willing to lay down their lives for the glory of the state and for Islam itself. We are in the process of informing your parents that unless an exorbitant amount of ransom is sent to us in three days, we will slit your throats and send your heads back to your father." He then turned and left.

Gambler saw a tear in the eye of the young lady. She was sixteen years old and very enamored that an attractive man would be led to follow her by means of seductive gestures and positionings. Her ego was so flattered that she did not want to see him die. That night she crept out of her tent with a knife and cut their bonds and gags. She placed a finger to her lips to indicate silence and motioned them to follow her. She led them over the mountain trails through forested lands to a cave. Once inside, she said, "My name is Souvia. I am Koutar's step daughter. My father was both an Amok and a Juramentado. He was convinced that his life meant more to the Moro state and the religion of Islam than it did to him. He sacrificed it in the senseless wars against the Americans that caused the bloodshed Koutar cries about. My mother put a kris to her breast at his funeral because she loved him more than she loved the state or religion. She wanted to leave this insanity and live a normal life, as a woman, who can make this life count, instead of looking for a heaven that offered nothing to a female child, not even the love of a father." She asked to be interred by the Americans and given political asylum.

They traveled for three days and followed the course of a river within the cavern's walls. The cave ended at the emptying of the river into a lake. From there they made their way to the American Embassy and home to Donny. He was in a rage when he had heard what had happened and wanted to wipe the Moros' stronghold off of the map. Tagura cautioned him against taking a path that would destroy the value of the Concord and render the progress as meaningless. Donny agreed and wondered how the lesson could be taught without violence.

Ambler presented a solution: The teens could handle it. If Souvia could lead them back through the cave with films of battle scenes along with appropriate tape recordings to create the sounds of battle and create the impression of mass movements of troops and equipment, the Moros might be scared out of their aggression. The question arose as to where this equipment could be obtained; Ambler had an answer, the museum had many exhibits that could be filmed if they were not already filmed. The screens would be painted to resemble the backgrounds against which they were placed. This had to be done, at least, a week before the attack. Souvia was instrumental in selecting appropriate sites upon which to project the films, as well as helping the kids to get through the cave. After each session prickly brambles and odiferous plants, along with slabs of meat to attract carnivores, were placed at the mouth of the cave.

When "D Day" came, the Moros ran. Koutar tried in vain to stop them. After all, he did not want his sultanate to crumble. A group of teens, who had become as disillusioned as Souvia cornered him, trying to stop the flight; they tore off his pants and underclothes, so that if he wanted to continue his ranting program, he would have to do so without his clothes.

The entire process was filmed and sent to Bobby and Bruno. This also served as a justification for a museum that lauded peacetime movements during the destructive phases of war.

Chapter 2

Koutar was fit to be tied. He wanted revenge against the kids that had staged a battle with films and noises. He did not want to appear as the instigator of violence so he thought he'd try government agencies to find what deeds he could bring down on the family, known as Clippingbird. He found out about the connection between Mictal and the Senator and Congressman through a lobby group and about Mictal's faith and belief in his friend. Any data that surfaced about Donny's involvement in crime was shaded by the good done in the Philippines on both of his trips and his work in establishing the museum. The stories about his participation in murders were shaded by his not being a direct participant, such as the Mob's decision to kill the loan shark's liaison because he had made the work of the Mob public. They also sat together and tried to find some connection to the murder of Don Enrico Dombrero and could not come up with any evidence that linked Donny to the Mob. They then came across Dominic's and Penny's names living under government protection. They traced the raid to Andorra and learned about the rescue and catching significant mobsters. They also explored some of the connections to the Irish Mob, as well as the Russian Mafia. The role Bobby played in having Isaac's sentence reduction fail to take place, and the murder of Tandry Obrits were thoroughly explored; further investigations were also attempted.

Being unable to unlock any suspicious behavior, Koutar began to go back into American history to trace back to the Pan Indian Movement and into the past life goal Donny had pursued. He was able to find out from his schoolboy years that he would set up kids by arranging liaisons with prostitutes and had dealings with pimps. He also came upon mention of Ms. Pitressin and her principal husband:

the fictitious rape was reawakened and sworn to have occurred. The Senator and Congressman both agreed to cooperating with Koutar in bringing this scoundrel to justice. Another avenue of vengeance was establishing criminal interest in the relationship between Scherlien and Bobby and Penny and Dominic.

What interest Mr. and Ms. Barringer and Mr and Ms. Umbriano had in working with kids, and why they chose to expose them to the prison system was a curious question. A couple of Moro agents posed as government officials, seeking to keep the prison eligible to receive moneys went to the "reading room" where privileged prisoners could read at night was inspected. The last resident to enjoy this freedom was Isaac Delfino. A note was made to investigate further broken boards in the wall. The closeness of the ventilating system to the fan and to this room were also noted. The deaths of the Italian and Irish residents were compared to the time of death of the Bulgar. These were also compared to the times of the visits of the law students. No conclusive evidence was discovered, but the ground was fertile for the stretching of truth and wielding it into a potential pattern. Koutar was doing his homework, and the Senator and Congressman were pleased at the data he had retrieved through his agents. An inspection of the roof revealed imprints of runners that may have belonged to a helicopter. An attempt to subpoena Isaac Delfino brought no new information, as he was buttoned up at the time. However a cuff link with the initials BC on it was found on the roof.

The Barringers and Umbrianos were forewarned to file lawsuits with the Civil Liberties Union and to go to the offices of those protecting their immunities against disclosures of their pasts. One of the Moro agents went to Chris' school and spread rumors that his parents had a checkered past. When he brought this up to Dominic and Penny, Dominic filed suit, but he also had fun with him. He put on a mask and bought a checkered shirt from a costume shop. At night, as the agent emerged from a bar to pursue a seductive lady (Penny), he was tripped by a tall, costumed figure who ordered him to take his shirt off, put on the checkered shirt, and lie down. Chris and Penny began to play checkers on his back. Every time they made a jump, a sock dipped in barbecue sauce and pepper was put in his mouth, and mustard was put on his eyebrows.

Koutar was feeling frustrated and decided to force Mictal to talk about the criminal background he knew about. One day, he was snatched by two huge men while he was returning to his office at work. He was taken to an abandoned junkyard and tied to a chair in the office. Koutar sat before him with torture instruments within his reach. What Koutar failed to notice was that Mictal had a camera ring that took pictures of all that he underwent. A clamp was put on his index finger and connected to a wire that ended in a clamp that was attached to his Achilles Tendon. His foot was brought near to a flame, and every time he flexed his foot his index finger was pulled in the direction of another flame; the pulls got closer to the flame with denial. At the same time a wire was attached to his eyebrows, and his lids were held open while a jagged piece of glass kept being moved closer to his eye. He resisted these threats, and more pain was added. His lips were pulled with pliers. His efforts to remain silent were heroic. He was not sure how much he could resist.

Suddenly, the silent entertainment was interrupted by the blast of a tommy gun. Donny stood there holding the smoking gun. The Arabs ran, except for Koutar. He ducked behind a counter and began firing a rifle that he had picked up. Donny aimed at a picture of a centaur that hung above Koutar, and it fell on him with his head sticking out at the level of the gluteal portion of the horse. Mictal was cut loose and joined his comrade. He asked how Donny had found him. He said that he suspected that Mictal would be a target since the frequent contacts from the Senator and Congressman had doubled in the last two weeks. He had coated Mictal's shoes with honey and ipecac while he was swimming at the office pool. The camera ring was sent to Bruno and Bobby. Mictal was surprised that he did not detect the aroma of the mixture. A laser was used to trace the mixture. The Senator and the Congressman were both sent the picture of Koutar's face in proximity with the horse's posterior.

The return of the accusation of the rape was managed by a dual methodology. The evidence that Bruno had brought forward at the initial trial was re-invoked to show that Donny could not possibly have done it, and Penny denied that such an attack ever took place and submitted the statement to the lawyers. However, Koutar had also taken pictures of the proceedings that showed that Donny was capable of resorting to violence by wielding a gun to enforce his getting things done the way he wanted. Donny attempted to counter this with the argument that he took deliberate measures to see that no one was hurt in rescuing Mictal. He also stressed that no violence was used in breaking up the Moros' attempted attack. This could also be interpreted as using the threat of violence by a court. Likewise, the use of the Pan Indian Doctrine to control the Principal and Ms. Pitressin could be interpreted as a controlling act, which held the connotation of an abusive act.

Koutar could see that he was getting nowhere. He decided on a new tactic. He would attack his daughter and the boys through the newspapers, then use this as a basis for attacking the American role in the Philippines. He started out by stating that his daughter had forgotten the Moslem teachings about comeliness in the female/male relationships because she was flattered by the male attention showed by Rambler. These boys were brought up in the American tradition of thinking they were better than anyone and that all women threw themselves at Americans because of the wealth they flaunted to women of other nationalities. He felt that these spoiled brats deserved beheading, but he had planned to allow the parents to pay a ransom for their lives, which the Greedy Americans owed the Islamic Filipinos for disrupting their country with their greed for land and money, both of which Americans enjoyed in plentitude and coveted from weaker, poorer nations whom they could subdue. This was also made more obvious by their forging an alliance with the Filipino Christians. However, he was thankful that Amoks and Juramentados were trained to be willing to sacrifice themselves for their nation and Islam.

Needless to say, Souvia was infuriated at the temerity of these accusations and turned to Donny and Bobby. They advised that the accusations be returned measure for measure via a national TV debate. However, Souvia would have to develop some anger management skills so that Koutar could not trip her up by letting her emotions get in the way. She learned to stick to her topic and to spot the emotional and physical signs of anger and to pause and halt the escalation.

Souvia caught herself getting angry and paused to regain her bearings. She then replied that Koutar was her stepfather, not her father. Her real sire was a devout Amok and Juramentado, who was afraid to leave his wife husbandless and his daughter fatherless. Koutar worked on him stating that he would take his place, while the father spent eternity with Mohammed in Paradise. The devotee of Islam entered an American army camp under the guise of a white flag. He opened his coat when he was near the munitions dump, but a quick witted guard saw the dynamite and the father about to light the fuse and shot first.

Koutar felt he was the adult and had the right to speak first. He went through his spiel and could see Souvia getting angrier and angrier. However, she paused and regained her cool, then answered him. She stated that her mother took a kris to her breast at the funeral and that Koutar's teachings of comeliness consisted of schooling her in the ways of seducing young men and enticing them into her father's camp to be executed, ransomed, or both. She had seen enough executions and seen enough killings when ransoms were paid, to not trust Koutar. She did not want to see a young boy, whose only crime was to be attracted to her, die needlessly. She knew she had to go with him or be killed by Koutar.

Koutar was so enraged that he charged at Souvia and got his foot caught in a waste basket. The announcer was so overcome with laughter that he had to leave the stage. The audience joined him in his mirth. The Senator and Congressman turned off their TVs.

Koutar left the stage with a red face and hobbling with his foot in a garbage can. He went straight to Souvia's dressing room and hit her with a heavy clay ashtray. She lost consciousness and had to be rushed to the hospital. She was found to be suffering a severe concussion and did not regain consciousness for two days. In spite of his sage advice, Donny was enraged and went to Koutar's hotel room with a bullwhip.

Koutar opened the door to face the cat o'nine tails across his face; he put his arms up to shield his face, and the whip tore through his shirt sleeve to the skin and drew blood. Donny switched ends and grasped the whip handle with his hand. He cracked it across Koutar's nose. This was followed by the loud cracking of bone and more blood.

In backing away, Koutar tripped and fell. Donny advanced on him and began kicking his ribs. Three men burst in through the door upon the complaint of a neighbor and held Donny back while Koutar groaned and coughed up more blood. He rose to his feet and phoned for an ambulance to take him to the hospital. The security guards were still holding Donny down. He was still struggling to get more of a piece of Koutar, who kept his distance, out of fear. Donny was escorted to jail, and Koutar filed a police report from the hospital. Unfortunately for Donny, the whole episode was filmed, a service the hotel provided for its guests.

Becky and Souvia visited Donny in jail and let him know that Koutar and the government officials were charging him with Felonious Assault. Bobby and Bruno also came to see him and let him know that all the material he had filed with them had been sent to the court. Becky and Souvia both kissed his cheek for being their hero and the hero of all suppressed women. He smiled, but he knew that grim days were ahead of him. His enemies had worked hard to get a case.

Chapter 3

The Clippingbirds made their farewells to the Philippines and Mindanao to return to the United States. Ambler and Bantu vowed to stay in touch and make a decision about whether or not they wanted to marry, and Souvia left with them to stay with them until she reached adulthood. Koutar left for Washington to confer with the Congressman and Senator about building his case. They saw their venture, as similar as the case against Al Capone for income tax evasion, back in the thirties. Tagura, Brontos, Captain Adalos, Bantu and the entire Mindanaoan village agreed to appear in court on Donny's behalf and sent written statements about his integrity, respect for people's customs and manner of conducting business, efforts to direct business peacefully, and whatever character references would be needed. Also mentioned were the efforts at working for union between the tribes and the pirates and supporting the youth in bringing families back together again. These were corroborated by written statements, visual tapes, audio tapes, and governing body testimony.

However, the prosecution was also active in gathering its materials to show a violent Donny that only had in mind an eye for an eye mentality in interpreting the Pan Indian Movement that went back to Donny's boyhood. Testimony was dug up about his schooldays, during which he not only taught the preppies to fight back, but also exploited them by exposing them to prostitutes, gamblers, and other criminal types. The heartless manner in which he punished Ms. Pitressin and her husband/principal and those who were harassing Randal (Rodin and Liana's son) was brought up. They also dug up the many times Becky, Ki, and Donny's father had to intervene to divert him from violence and retaliation. Neighbors had overheard the many interventions and were drafted to testify, whether or not they wanted to do so.

A crucial strategy was decided upon. The defense had elected to go for a jury trial. This would throw responsibility for deciding guilt or innocence upon the American public for several legal policy decisions. Does changed behavior merit giving a defendant another chance? Or does the behavior determine a right and responsibility by society to exact punishment for what has been done to others? Is there a validity to considering what a man has worked for, aside from what he has done? At what point does society have a right to exact vengeance? Do Congressmen and other legislators need to be present at trials/hearings to see the workings of the laws that are passed out of their houses?

Jury selection was done while Donny was in jail. People that were sent home were those that had experience with Indian affairs, such as reservations, choosing officials for reservations, those with gambling problems, former Mafia victims or beneficiaries, anyone affiliated with the prison system. One of the areas that was neglected were former prep school students. Bobby and Bruno saw this as a way to get jurors that didn't like bullies on Donny's side. As a result, evidence that Donny had shown the students how to stand up and fight their own battles was brought out and updated for presentation by the defense.

The prosecution also devised strategies to bring out the hatred and violent sides to Donny's persona. The prosecutor paid police to put Donny in the same cell with aggressive provocative arrestees, who would wile away time by trying to pick fights in jail. There were a lot of Skinheads, neo Nazis, white supremacists, Aryan Brotherhood members from former incarcerations in the same cell as Donny. Bruno came to visit him and warned him that these types were placed in his cell to test his mettle; he was advised to recall his teachings to Souvia, who was a frequent visitor along with his wife and kids. A visit was organized for Tagura and Bantu. He was glad to see them. Bantu had decided to come to the States and to marry Ambler. He and Donny were able to divert some of the inter-jail tension by discussing the big culture shock Bantu was facing. Despite the efforts of the prosecutor, Donny was able to maintain a balanced personality.

Bantu, with the teaching of Ambler, was planning on completing a GED exam and trying to attend school as a journalist, while working for a local newspaper. Donny felt he was trying to bite off more than he could chew and advised him to slow the process down because building a relationship also involved choosing what you like and what you're good at doing; part of it also involved them getting to know each other. Bantu took this in and agreed to think about it and to discuss it with Ambler, who was itching to have a baby.

After the visit was over, Donny was returned to the grimness of incarceration by a Skinhead putting his arm around him with a knife at the vicinity of his Carotid Artery whispering that if Donny didn't get the key from the guard, he'd cut his throat open. The gambler noticed that the guard wore his billy club on his belt next to the position where he wore the key. He called the guard over and grabbed the club from off of his belt and hit his would be assailant in the jaw with it, exposing the hand with a knife in it. The guard shot the instrument of death out of his hand. Donny handed the billy club back to the guard, who thanked him. When he told Bobby about it, his brother and lawyer sent for a newspaper reporter to get an interview for the paper. Donny was the "Hero for Peace in the House of War". The prosecutor saw it as an opportunity to expose the gambler as a person of violence, who resorts to it in times of stress because it had become second nature to him. The divergent views were used as criteria for dismissing or retaining potential jurors. The questions of where the prisoner got the knife and why it was not found on search were also raised but not answered.

The examination of the selection of exhibits for the museum brought forth another issue that the defense would employ: One of the preppies that Donny had taught to fight off attackers went on to participate in the Vietnam War. At Da Nang, he got separated from his outfit and was in the unenviable position of being on the ground and separated from his weapon. He also found himself facing the bayonets of the officer in charge of a company and a lower officer. Remembering a fighting technique he learned from Donny, he kicked out at the closest soldier to him so that he would fall into the other one. Moving as swiftly as it would take to save his life, he got hold of one rifle and stabbed the one nearest him in the neck and held the other at bay with the gun. The survivor turned out to be the company commander. With the bayonet at the officer's neck, he bade him tell the rest of his company to drop their arms and surrender, which they did at the same time the preppie's company rejoined him. He got a medal, and a place in the museum.

The skinhead who was thwarted circulated his dissatisfaction to the other prisoners. At bedtime, he had several cellmates dancing around Donny's bed and imitating war whoops. One got close and took his shank out and cut off a hank of hair from Donny's head. The scalped area bled profusely, while the scalper boasted about his prowess in scalping the scalper and making up for all the times it was done to the white man. Donny tried to divert his thinking to avoid the appearance of one controlled by rage. However, at breakfast he noticed that there was a space next to the scalper's place. He got hot oatmeal in a bowl and untied his shoe lace and went to sit at the table, acting as if there were no hard feelings, as he reached the table, he tripped over the shoe lace, and the scalding cereal spilled in the man's face. Donny immediately picked up a napkin and began to wipe the man's face. In the wiping process, some oatmeal got in the poor fellow's eyes. Later in the day, an Aryan Brotherhood member offered Donny the hand of friendship. Donny took it and clasped it, but told him that he would not allow himself to be part of a group. He also took him aside and explained why he could not afford any group affiliation. He did not say anything about how repugnant the philosophy was to him. The scalper let the incident pass as an example of "What goes around comes around," The prosecution was hard put to find any retaliation in the gesture, especially since the scalper was given an uncertain warning not to be a snitch.

At any rate, Donny was presenting himself to his fellow prisoners as a "righteous dude". He would not run to authorities for protection, but he would not take any guff either. He would seek his solutions within the realm of his peers and avoid whining to the authorities to protect him from injustices. In keeping with this philosophy, he recalled the times he and Craine, or he and Patrick, or he and Rodin all made each others' pain their own and stood together. This happened at Masada, Thermopylae, and Shiloh. Enmity breeds friendship because of bonding where there is a common foe. Atrocity is stopped by numbers blocking it through resistance. The numbers make its injustice visible. This is why support is sought for an opinion and/or an action. The methodology used is related to the attempts the opposing party uses to suppress the change that is being offered.. He discussed this view with his brother and Bruno, who agreed to look into this interpretation and where it led. He remembered the motto of Alexander Dumas' *Three Musketeers*: "One for all, and All for one." Children were taught these dictums as the basis of working together to build a better world. Why was it evil to use the same violence to which one was exposed to teach the ones perpetrating the violence that they were creating a vicious circle, whose extrication meant wiping out everyone?

He was not even sure that his application of these precepts was an accurate statement or a function of his own pain and, perhaps, misperception. He thought of the miscreant antics of Ms. Pitressin towards her daughter and him, as well as the attempt of the principal and her to lash out at Donny and Penny. Did such acts fall into the category of "Forgiving them, for they do not know what they do," or "Vengeance is mine?" Donny could not fathom on which pathway/he could direct himself. What was the motivation of Tecumseh's Pan Indian Movement? Did his own anger act to distort his perception of the meaning of it, or was it a righteous anger that could only be expressed to stop an unending wrong?

Becky, Souvia, as well as Penny and Scherlien were frequent visitors and encouraged him by reminding of the good he had done and how The Diced Chick provided employment and income for the Blackfoot tribe by virtue of Donny's Purchase Agreement. One of the accusations against him was that he took advantage of people with gambling addictions. Scherlien showed him a document stating that he had saved Randal from his addiction. The document was signed by Liana and by him and notarized. It was sent to Bobby and Bruno.

A policeman was brought in unconscious with a loss of much blood. He was shipped to the nearest ER. Donny saw his wife and children at the station in tears and unable to function because of the anxiety attack that became superimposed on their grief. He motioned to the guard and stated he was a universal donor and would give blood so that the officer would be able to take care of his family. A guard accompanied him to the hospital and was chained to the non-donating arm. After it was over, the guard tried to smuggle some of the cookies and juice given to donors in his pockets. In the police car Donny picked his pocket and ate a second helping of chocolate cookies and a bottle of orange juice. When he told Becky about the incident, she pointed her finger at him scoldingly and laughed. The officer lived. He and his family agreed to testify for Donny in court.

Donny had grown up on the wrong side of the street, and because of this he instinctively learned that if he would stay in jail, instead of going out on bond, he could begin an organization of his defense by observing how his jailers related to him. He and Bobby both recognized that the prosecutor's office was trying to railroad him into displaying violent behavior then linking it with crimes of violence, such as the death of Tambry Obrits and the escape from Andorra. They also wanted to tie him into the death of Don Dombrero.

Donny was getting stir crazy. He had his bail paid and was in a restaurant with Souvia, Ambler, and Becky. He saw Koutar talking with two men at another table. Neither of them saw him. Donny suspected that the other men were the Senator and Congressman. He made a mental note to have Mictal check into this. Koutar had an angry expression on his face and banged his fist on the table. The Senator turned red and turned to see if anyone had witnessed the scene. He blanched as he saw Donny. The three of them got up and left.

Mr. Clippingbird phoned Mictal, who already knew about the conference and who the conferees were. He informed him that they were hatching a plot to have Donny diagnosed with a sociopathic disorder that consisted of getting a thrill out of violence. They were in the process of finding a psychiatrist that agreed with them.

Donny started looking for a psychiatrist or psychologist that would stress the good works he had done as a sign of regret and an attempt to seek forgiveness for his wrongful behavior; thus, he wanted to turn around the image of getting a thrill out of the violence by showing that this image caused him pain that he was trying to alleviate. He also wanted to illustrate that the violence occurred as a means of achieving noble ends by engaging the resistance, who would accept change no other way than being beaten. He illustrated that the noble drives of men became policies through opposition being forced to yield. Examples he gave were the American Civil War, India's struggle for independence from Britain, and the evolution of a civilized nation of Australia from a penal colony.

Bobby and Bruno took these examples and likened Donny's struggles to do good works as parallel to them. He likened the struggle to unite the tribes to Lincoln's statement that, "A house divided cannot stand." It took the North and South depleting their manpower and resources to see that all men had to have the same rights for the union to survive. There was no room for the acceptance of slavery in a union that preached Democracy. It took violence to show the Australians that a nation cannot exist where men pillage, rape, and kill, and kill each other. To establish order men had to decide that law and not might makes right prevails. The advocates of violent rule had to be confronted to establish what the rule would be. In India, Ghandi had to show the British Empire that they were making other men's homes their homes by making the English intrusion less homey.

Bobby and Bruno proposed the thesis that because violent means were used to achieve noble ends, it did not necessarily follow that the person was evil. After all World War II was allegedly fought to "make the world safe for democracy." To join ranks with the majority of the world's population, Donny became part of the instrumentation of movement toward brotherhood of man by displaying the moments when people reached out to one another. This instrumentation was the museum, a capture of Man's finer moments in relation to other men. This cooperative step had been mentioned in many literary efforts that were expressed as a byproduct of violent moves, such as in Margaret Mitchell's *Gone with the Wind*. Didn't Scarlett T. O'Hara preserve Tara, her home by working together with poor whites and Afro-Americans? Did not this love for mankind follow the blood bath called the Civil War?

As part of the thesis that the lawyers were striving to create, the intertwining of justice, vengeance, and political turmoil had to be considered. Concentration camps created a class of survivors of terror and victims that were killed for what they were, not what they did. This class was embittered and demanded justice, to which they were entitled, but what of the enemy, that also consisted of people that were only obeying orders and were trying to rebuild their lives in a moral way. Are such people entitled to a system of justice that takes into account that changes are being made? Judges are elected officials in local jurisdictions. They are subject to render their decisions on how the populace in the area views the severity of the crime if they want to be reelected. There is reason for the public to be affected. But the judicial Department of government is supposed to be the interpreter of the law, not a mirror of public sentiment.

By being the public mirror, judges forget that by catering to those who seek revenge, they cause them to forget that forgiveness allows the sufferer to let go of unhealthy rages. The anger remains, and the one punished may have to suffer for more than what he/she did and have their efforts to change be ignored.

In order to show that the court policies and legal system could be in need of revision one must consider motivation of behavior in its entire context; the legal team pointed out several cases in which justice was not served, and in which guilt was questionable because the basis of the guilty finding was emotional, rather than factual. In 1913 a young girl was murdered in the state of Georgia. Her name was Mary Phagan. A Jewish man by the name of Leo Frank was found guilty and electrocuted for this crime. After his death an Afro-American janitor confessed to the killing. In Cleveland, Ohio, in the 1950's a doctor, Sam Sheppard, was found guilty of murdering his wife. He kept talking about a one armed man that was employed by the Sheppards that might be a potential suspect for the killing. Dr Sheppard served several years in prison and was pardoned for doing voluntary work in medical areas. The last that this writer heard, he spent his last years playing the role of a wrestler for carnivals. Posthumously, his son is trying to clear his name. A prisoner with one arm confessed to the crime on his deathbed. In the wake of the Russian Revolution a payroll at a factory was robbed and a guard was killed. Two Italian immigrants, Sacco and Vanzetti, were accused and found guilty of the robbery/murder, not because facts proved it, but because they had socialist leanings. They languished in prison for seven years, despite worldwide letters of protest. Then they were electrocuted. To this day no guilt was established beyond a reasonable doubt. The fear of the spread of communism was what convicted them.

The rationale behind presenting the errors that the legal system had caused was to cause the jurors to realize that basing their findings on the past was also an error because Donny had changed as he grew and got exposed to more people and more ideas. They would be convicting another person if they relied on the past as the whole story. He had become a man that could help people expand in their thinking to include changes that would be best for the majority and the minority. He was forced to make use of methods he learned in the past because he was dealing with people that wanted to cling to the negative view of human beings and to treat them accordingly. In order to get them to alter their views, they had to see that the thinking had to change, and this would only happen if the old ways were stopped by the old methods. Hence, they were forced to listen to a new alternative.

The prosecution felt that "a leopard cannot change his spots." They thought the new Donny and the old Donny were the same. He had learned to hate the prejudice of the white man and to fight it by giving the same as he got. For this reason, he tried to turn the Caucasian's weakness against him, the way he had used alcohol against the Indian. This, they felt, became his way of fighting back. The way he fought the white man became the way he fought, period. What he did to get the Mafioso killed was the same way he tricked the preppies to spend their money on gambling and prostitutes. It was the same way he had gotten revenge against Ms. Pitressin and her principal/husband. It was also the same way he had led Tandry Obrits to his death. The use of the weakness of greed was a way to trap his victims from his boyhood to his adulthood.

Chapter 4

Danny figured that since the newspapers were instrumental in bringing about the above convictions, that he could use them to his advantage. He asked his lawyers to dig up the stories about how he and his family had learned to communicate as a part of the preparations for their trip to the Philippines, and the story of the preppie that became a war hero in Vietnam because of what Donny had taught him about self defense. He also stated that part of what he did to Ms. Pitressin and the principal was to give them a chance to learn how to earn an honest living instead of trying to squeeze money out of people, as they did his father. He also helped Penny find her own way to support herself and Chris by holding her mother's greed in check. This and turning the mob away from taking advantage of Randal La Monde's addiction to gambling helped turn the young man away from losing his money to a profession that benefited society, that of medicine. The owner of the gambling establishment had done much to benefit society and felt that the public should know this. Bruno was the one who approached the papers with these stories.

Another point of view was also given to the newspapers: If Donny had to be held to task for his past angry, violent behavior, why did not Ms. Pitressin and the principal be held accountable for devising and presenting a false accusation of rape that cost an innocent youngster to have an education sacrificed to satisfy their prejudices and need to create a victim? The lawyers were, at first, reluctant to use this data because it had the form of an accusation from a case that had already been heard and resolved. However, Donny pointed out that they were not being brought to trial twice, but he was being tried once. Just as telephone conversations or lie detector test results are barred from the courtroom, but are brought up and banned so that the jury hears them, so might the false accusation be used. Besides, the information was to be given to the newspapers, not the court. Bruno went ahead with dispensing the information.

The prosecution also went to the news media. They were asking why did Koutar have to be attacked with a bull whip instead of brought before the law for putting Souvia in the hospital. Was this the act of someone that agreed to work within the law? Who had killed Tandry Obrits and why was the law not approached rather than having a gun battle? Another question that was posed was why did the guard have to be killed in rescuing the Robinsons from Port Arthur and why were people with criminal records part of the team that carried out the rescue? The choice of Mictal as an employee in a strategic position was questioned. Was he chosen because he owed Donny something for his part in the scheme to attract Penny Pitressin to him by putting Donny down? Why did Mictal not cooperate with the relatives in the government?

The battle between the defense and prosecution seemed to be about even. A recent episode of violence had to be produced which would inflame the jury to a rage that would attest to Donny's nature being one of a violence prone individual that did not mind taking a human life if the person interfered with his plans. If this suspicion could be verified, they could approach the media with the story. They began to research the Red Man's past and present to find the piece of data for which they were searching.

The news media created their own incident. A reporter referred to Bobby wanting to be a consigliera for the Mob. For this reason he said that he began romancing La Dona, who at the time was Scherlien. He hinted that there must be some corruption going on for him to be represented by such an unsavory reputationed lawyer. Donny warned him to desist because the counsel, about whom he was speaking, was his brother. The reporter pushed the item further and implied that growing up on a reservation could generate hatred for whites that could push one to criminality to get revenge. Donny warned him once more not to impugn the younger brother he had raised. The reporter went on talking about the potential for crookedness and took a picture of Donny's face that was beginning to show signs of anger. Donny yanked the camera out of his hand stomped on it. When the reporter protested in anger, Danny hit him in the nose. The cracking of the bone and blood flow was seen by another camera man, who took the picture. His camera was also snatched and crushed. He was also given a telling blow to the rib cage that gave off another cracking sound. Both blows made the morning papers. Bobby and Bruno were furious at Donny's impulsivity, but Bobby remembered the struggles the brothers had in growing up. However, this initiated an enmity with the press. The counselors tried to point out the unfairness of the attack and also tried to establish that the incident was deliberately perpetrated. No connection could be made between the prosecutor and the reporters until a known informant that the police used stated that he saw money exchanged between the two reporters and a member of the prosecution's staff. A rival newspaper wrote the story, but Donny had to bear responsibility for breaking one man's nose and the other's ribs, even though damage control had been achieved. The two cameras were not deemed very useful, and the reporters tried to file a lawsuit.

The lawsuit turned out to be a draw. The reporters were proven by the informant's testimony to be engaged in a paid harassment and provocation endeavor. They did not lose their jobs, but Donny did not have to pay for their cameras. He did have to pay for their broken bones. Newspapers were not very sympathetic towards Donny in soliciting stories on his behalf. He did not look for their help either. Bruno and Bobby flooded the public with news about the newspapers' role in the Sacco and Vanzetti, Sheppard .and Frank cases. Once again, where Donny stood was hard to surmise.

The role of emotionality on influencing judges' attitudes was also brought into play. Bruno and Bobby began to study the views of the appellate judicial structure and began to look for support if it would be needed. They even began to probe the State Supreme Court for support. The testimony of the state informer played a big role in these attempts. This case would not be a clear cut disposition of justice.

Since he had committed another felonious act, Donny had to return to jail. The inmates did the same thing they always did: agitate a newcomer to put him to the attention of the guards. Donny had become "A sadder but a wiser man." He ignored those that poked fun at him, reflected back remarks that were made to him or about himself. The third part of his self sustenance was to deliver needed violent retaliation where none could see or hear it.

For instance, he encountered the skinhead that tried to scalp him. The next day, he untied his shoelaces again when he went to chow. Again he was carrying hot oatmeal in a large vat to replenish the supply for the men. As he passed the neo-Nazi's table, he tripped and spilled hot cereal in his face. The man stood up in a rage and picked up a chair. Donny merely swerved to his side for a few seconds, enough for the skinhead to get a view of the shank he carried with him.

The message came across that Donny wanted no trouble, but if it came to him, he wouldn't run. The skinhead and several others that had tormented Donny also got the message. This opened the door to respect and friendship. Donny did not expect this, and it kept the prosecution from gaining alliances with the residents in the form of reduced sentences to be snitches or to create testimony of violent behavior. In fact they agreed to testify that Donny didn't bother anyone unless he was methodically or cruelly provoked. He did not have to carry the shank any more. He also was put in a position to help some of the inmates to find jobs, sources of financial aid for school and/or training, recommending therapists and therapeutic programs that would avoid incarceration, and setting up appointments for legal aid for the cases.

Bobby and Bruno had a hard time getting the media to publicize these deeds. Hence they interviewed the residents selectively and made DVDs, to be shown to the judge in chambers. The prosecutor was also present and objected to the pro-defendant evidence being presented to the judge before the hearing. The lawyers got it overruled because all the negative data was presented by the newspapers and other media before the hearing also. He did ask that it be repeated at the time of the hearing, to which Bobby and Bruno agreed.

Donny was trying to have an answer for every bit of negativity that the prosecution dug up on him. Koutar paid someone to attack him, and he had a hidden camera and was able to film it. Koutar was visited by the Congressman and the Senator, who wanted him to stay out of the trial because he was doing more harm than good. In fact they advised him to go back to the Philippines and handle his own affairs. They reminded him that his sultanate was crumbling while he was getting into affairs about which he had little or no knowledge. Thus, the prosecutions lost one of its allies.

Donny was beginning to get worried because of the hard time he was having with the media. He was pondering finding the basis of a lawsuit for not publishing news accurately or honestly. Bobby warned him that he was only provoking their wrath and making things worse. He suggested going to the magazines because he did not antagonize them as much as he did the newspapers. *Life Magazine* agreed to do a story on him, stressing the good over the bad. The editor that made the promise was a member of the Robinson family he had been part of rescuing from Port Arthur. The article was an autobiography and pointed how the evil side of Donny came from the abuse at the reservation. But it also stressed that he struggled with his fellow Man to forgive his trespasses and tried to create good from bad, starting with his contribution to build the museum and that he formed alliances with true friends for which he was willing to risk his health and safety.

Donny was trying to find a way to beat the newspapers and ally himself with other forms of the media, such as *Life Magazine* when a golden opportunity almost smacked him in the face. The reporter ,whose nose he had broken had lost his job because of the publicity the paper had gotten in the exchange of money between the prosecution and the news hawk. He saw Donny at a coffee shop and started to give him a dirty look. The Blackfoot approached him, saying that they did not have to remain enemies. He then suggested that he write the story about his struggle with anger and submit it to *Life* and see if he could get a job as a contract writer. The man apologized to Donny for the nasty remarks about his brother and submitted the letter.

The writer shook Donny's hand and agreed to try it and to also let the other newspapers know of his generosity. *Life* was enthusiastic about the article and agreed to hire the reporter to write an autobiography.

Donny related the life experiences and the people he came to know and love, as well as hate, to his former enemy. He told him how he had to take care of his little brother amidst the scorn and ridicule he had to endure at the hands of the white boys, and how he met Corlando and LeBere and how they won him and Bobby over. He recalled his experiences with the preppies: how he taught them to defend themselves, and how he scorned them and separated them from their money. He related the scheme dreamt up by Ms. Pitressin and the principal and his experiences in the Merchant Marines. He spoke about how he was torn between the hatred he had experienced and the love he experienced through his stepfather, Ki, and Becky. He went on to say he let himself be dominated by the hatred when he felt betrayed or he or his friends were victimized. This led him to distort Tecumseh's doctrine.

The distortion made him permanent enemies and a group of loyal friends. These friends came to each other's aid and used whatever means were necessary to preserve their lives and relationships. They worked with government agencies. One idea that was passed down was to preserve the moments of human love that went beyond the barriers of hatred that wars created or that had occurred in implementing the laws of competition to eliminate rivals. Donny had learned these firsthand when he sought out candidates for remembrance for the museum, and when he had worked in the Philippines to promote unity where there was divisiveness. He practiced what he preached for the sake of his children. If he had to resort to violence, it was in the nature of why the United States had fought in World War II to preserve Democracy. He posed the question of whether or not this was an example of a leopard not changing its spots. He asserted that he did change his spots so that his children would be able to work for a world free from the destructive elements that hatred and vengeance created in their wakes from the time that Cain slew Abel to the day his father had to kill children soldiers at Remagen. He also brought up elements of his own vengeful past in which he embraced the friendship of Penny and Mictal because they did not want to be connected with the evil, angry prejudice of their parents.

Now he felt that he had been granted his right to speak. However, he felt unsure about the tendencies of members of society to carry their angers into their administrations of justice and to use their numbers to put pressures on the judges. He had gone as far into the human psyche as he could. The rest was up to the courts.

The End

Author's Note:

I am not trying to debase American Law and its practices. I am trying to open our eyes to show that even with good intentions roads can be paved to Hell. We can create a Serbian minority that will slay all the Archduke Ferdinands or react emotionally to finding a target for our rages and blame him/her or them. What do we do when a Hitler emerges to seek his own sick vengeance? If we are, indeed, the guardians of Democracy, then let us guard it and not fall asleep on our laurels or let the impersonal doctrines of guilt and innocence that we invent to hide our anger from ourselves take over the responsibility of making not only just, but also morally responsible decisions; for all the decisions we make go further than the courtroom. They enter into our professional family, and neighborly lives as well.